A game of one-on-one

"You know you'll still beat me," Alison said after a pause.

"Even though I'm a cripple?" He said it again, on purpose this time, experimenting. He hadn't choked, had he? She still looked scared. "Huh?"

"Yes."

He looked at her. He waited. The silence lengthened.

"Even though you're a cripple," she said finally. "Is that what you wanted me to say? Well, are you happy?"

He *was* happy. Harry was suddenly, gloriously, irrationally happy. "Yeah," he said. "I'll beat you. But that doesn't matter. It's not about winning." He spun around, heading closer to the basket. "Come on. I'll show you some moves. You're probably not as bad as you think you are. Attitude is real important in sports, and, to be frank, Queen Nerd, yours sucks. We can work on that."

After a minute, dazed, Alison followed Harry.

For my sister, Susan.
I love you.

SPEAK
Published by the Penguin Group
Penguin Group (USA) Inc., 345 Hudson Street, New York, New York 10014, U.S.A.
Penguin Group (Canada), 90 Eglinton Avenue East, Suite 700,
Toronto, Ontario, Canada M4P 2Y3 (a division of Pearson Penguin Canada Inc.)
Penguin Books Ltd, 80 Strand, London WC2R 0RL, England
Penguin Ireland, 25 St Stephen's Green, Dublin 2, Ireland
(a division of Penguin Books Ltd)
Penguin Group (Australia), 250 Camberwell Road, Camberwell, Victoria 3124, Australia
(a division of Pearson Australia Group Pty Ltd)
Penguin Books India Pvt Ltd, 11 Community Centre,
Panchsheel Park, New Delhi - 110 017, India
Penguin Group (NZ), 67 Apollo Drive, Mairangi Bay, Auckland 1311, New Zealand
(a division of Pearson New Zealand Ltd)
Penguin Books (South Africa) (Pty) Ltd, 24 Sturdee Avenue,
Rosebank, Johannesburg 2196, South Africa

Registered Offices: Penguin Books Ltd, 80 Strand, London WC2R 0RL, England

First published in the United States of America by Houghton Mifflin, 1994
Published by Speak, an imprint of Penguin Group (USA) Inc., 2007
Reprinted by agreement with the author.

10 9 8 7 6 5 4 3 2 1

Copyright © Nancy Werlin, 1994
All rights reserved
THE LIBRARY OF CONGRESS HAS CATALOGED THE HOUGHTON MIFFLIN EDITION AS FOLLOWS:
Werlin, Nancy.
Are you alone on purpose? / Nancy Werlin.
p. cm.
Summary: When two lonely teenagers, one the son of a widower rabbi and the other
the sister of an autistic twin, are drawn together by a tragic accident, they discover
they have more in common than they guessed.
ISBN: 0-395-67350-X (hc)
[1. Jews—Fiction. 2. Physically handicapped—Fiction. 3. Autism—Fiction.
4. Family life—Fiction. 5. Twins—Fiction.] I. Title.
PZ7.W4713 Ar 1994 93-37653
[Fic]—dc20 CIP AC

Speak ISBN 978-0-14-240777-6

Printed in the United States of America

are you
alone
on
purpose?

nancy werlin

speak

An Imprint of Penguin Group (USA) Inc.

ACKNOWLEDGMENTS

Many good friends and family members read this book, chapter by chapter, as I wrote it. When I got stuck or discouraged, they were always there with love, faith, and encouragement. My thanks to Elaine Werlin, Arnold Werlin, Miriam Werlin Rosenblatt, Max Romotsky, Victoria M. Lord, Barbara Hillers, Ellis O'Donnell, Gail Schulman, Jayne Yaffe, Anneke Kierstead, Juan Collas, Heather D. Atterbury, and J. Hannah Orden.

I'd also like to thank my mentor, the author Athena V. Lord, and my editor, Laura Hornik, for reading my first draft and seeing—and explaining to me—what the book could become.

ALISON • April

Later, Alison Shandling believed that she'd never have thought twice about Harry Roth—except to avoid him—if her father's great-uncle Simon hadn't died just when he did. Her father's brother, Dennis, called in the middle of dinner with the news of Simon's death, and Alison watched her father listen to it, watched his shoulders sag and then straighten. If you believed in fate, and Alison did, then with hindsight it was clear that this was the first event in some capricious cosmic conspiracy to upset her life, which she kept in precarious balance as it was.

Not to mention Harry Roth's life, about which, at the time, Alison knew next to nothing and cared even less.

But Alison did care about her family, and she

didn't know things were about to change. And when her father came back to the table, all four Shandlings sat quietly for a moment. Even Alison's twin brother, Adam.

"How old was Uncle Simon?" asked Alison's mother, finally.

"Ninety-three." Alison's father shook his head. "I don't know why I'm shocked....I haven't seen him since he showed up all on his own to see me get my Ph.D. Remember?"

"Like yesterday," said Mrs. Shandling. "I was pregnant, so your uncle and I were about equally mobile." She paused, her forehead wrinkling. "Jake, do you want to fly out to San Francisco tomorrow for the funeral?" She glanced at Adam. "I can manage here...."

"Dennis will go. But I don't see how I can," said Professor Shandling. "Joe Chin is scheduled to take his orals tomorrow. The date's been set for months."

Alison knew that was that. Her father took his teaching responsibilities seriously.

Alison's mother nodded. "You'll have to go say Kaddish for Uncle Simon tomorrow, instead."

"Yes." The professor half grimaced. "Betsy? Where's the synagogue in this town, anyway?"

Mrs. Shandling laughed. "You're asking me?"

Alison's father was grinning back at his wife ruefully when Alison asked, "What's Kaddish?"

There was a pause. Into it, Adam began a tune-less humming, keeping time with the low beat of his fork against his plate. Feeling her parents' eyes on her, Alison glanced at her brother, but, for once, her parents were focusing on Alison instead of him.

And Alison didn't like it.

Then her father pushed his plate of scallops away. "It's the Jewish prayer for the dead," he said. There was an odd note in his voice. Disapproval? She felt a little panicky. Professor Shandling never criticized Alison. Why should he? Alison was normal. She was not a problem.

She looked at him, and then at her mother. They looked back at her, their faces very still. "Well, I didn't know," she said quickly. "You always tell me to ask when I don't know something." She ate a scallop. "So I did."

For a few seconds, Alison could actually feel the heaviness of the silence in the kitchen. She glanced at her mother to try to gauge how angry or upset she was. Mrs. Shandling didn't get upset very often, and of course it was usually Adam—or something connected to Adam—that made her pace up and down and scream and cry. It was hard-ly ever Alison. Alison had been making sure of that for as long as she could remember.

Then her mother spoke. "Jake?" said Mrs. Shandling. Alison relaxed at her tone; it was thoughtful rather than agitated. "Maybe we should actually join a synagogue. The kids could go to Hebrew school, too. Even Adam. It's not too late."

And, from that moment, Alison's fate—and possibly Harry Roth's, as well—had been sealed.

The next Saturday the Shandlings began attending Sabbath services at Temple Ben Ezra. For Alison, the service consisted of two and a half hours of standing up and sitting down when everyone else did, and listening. A lot. Worst were the parts of the service that were in Hebrew. Alison had not realized that her parents read Hebrew.

Adam actually seemed to be having a good time. He hummed along with the singing and the chanting. And he loved the davening; he rocked away in perfect rhythm beside his father. That was a good moment, a rare moment. Alison caught her mother's eye, and they both smiled. It was incredible. All the men, swaying back and forth, muttering prayers under their breath, while Adam rocked right along with them. How wonderful for him, to suddenly find everybody else doing exactly what he did.

But Alison's amusement had faded by the time Rabbi Roth was three minutes into his sermon. Something about Jeremiah and the nuances of word order in biblical Hebrew. You had to consider grammatical subtleties, said Rabbi Roth, and pay close attention to underlying structure. You should cross-reference your conclusions with those of Talmudic scholars, he said.

Alison began counting the yarmulkes on the men's heads. On this side, fourteen white, forty-six black, and two funky crocheted ones. On the other side, starting from the front row, three white, and Harry Roth, bareheaded.

Harry Roth, from Alison's eighth-grade class, and from elementary school and countless playgrounds before that. Here. After a moment, Alison's mind began working. Rabbi Roth. Harry Roth. Of course.

Harry Roth, school bully. Rabbi's son. It was actually quite a good joke.

Rabbi Roth droned on.

"Pssst. Alison. Take this." Startled, Alison turned toward her father and, automatically, reached across her mother to take what he was offering. A Shandling Sphere. She turned the colorful little globe in her hands. On her father's other side, Adam was already working on one.

"It's not appropriate, Jake," Alison's mother whispered urgently. "This is a synagogue."

"The kids are dying of boredom," the professor whispered back. "So am I. Pompous windbag."

"But we wanted to do this!"

"In theory, yes. In practice…"

Alison tuned them out. She looked down at the Sphere and, comparing colors and shapes in her head, began trying to work its puzzle pieces into alignment. You needed to concentrate to do the Sphere. And if she concentrated, Alison wouldn't think about Harry.

Not that Harry mattered. Alison would simply keep out of his way here, just as she did in school.

The problem, of course, was that Adam was here too, and he made Alison feel very conspicuous, as if she were nine or ten instead of nearly fourteen, as if she were transported back to the time when she'd been in constant danger of having to defend her brother from other kids, nasty kids like Harry Roth.

She had hated Adam then.

The following Saturday's service was a repeat of the first, complete with Shandling Spheres during the sermon. This time, Alison accepted the Sphere from her father with reluctance. At breakfast, Alison's mother had said that it wasn't right. People would be watching, disapproving. But Professor Shandling had said that other people, such as his wife, could listen to the sermon if they pleased. He and his children would exercise their minds constructively. "Right, Alison?" he had said.

"Right, Dad," Alison had replied, dutifully.

Looking around now, she saw that several people were indeed watching, including Felicia Goren. Felicia was twisting in her seat, staring. Like Harry Roth, Felicia was in Alison's eighth-grade class, but Alison didn't really know her except by reputation. Alison mostly hung around with Paulina de Silva.

Felicia hung out with Harry's crowd.

Harry was up front again. Somehow, even his back looked bored. Alison supposed his father insisted that he sit up there. He was shifting a little in his chair. Alison's fingers twisted on the Sphere. She was too old for this; she really was. She wanted to give the Sphere back to her father, but he'd made such a big deal over it that she didn't dare. It would have focused attention on her.

After the service, the professor ushered the other Shandlings into the social hall next to the sanctuary, where small paper cups of wine, grape juice, and cake and challah were laid out. Alison kept an eye on Harry, Felicia, and the other kids her age. But, after grabbing some food, most of them disappeared into the little social hall, and Alison relaxed.

Last Saturday they had stayed only about ten minutes. "As we get to know people," Mrs. Shandling had said then, "we'll stay longer and chat with them." But people didn't seem any more eager to meet her parents this week than last, so Alison hoped they would leave soon. Adam had been quiet and unembarrassing so far, but you never knew. And with Harry Roth and those kids here...

And then Rabbi Roth was in front of them, smiling. "How do you do?" he said. "I saw you last week, didn't I? Are you new members?"

Alison tolerated being introduced. "You're twins?" Rabbi Roth asked kindly, looking from her to Adam, noticing, Alison knew, their red hair, their similar heights. "That's nice. I have a son about your age called Harry. He's around somewhere."

"He's in a couple of my classes at school," Alison said, to be polite.

"Ah," said the rabbi, "but he's not in Adam's classes?" He smiled at Adam, who was holding his hand in midair and watching his own fingers flicker.

Alison froze. Didn't the rabbi realize about Adam? "No," she said slowly. She met her mother's amazed eyes. Then she looked at her father. He was scowling at the rabbi.

"Adam and Alison don't go to the same school," said Mrs. Shandling, carefully, after a moment.

The rabbi frowned. "I know most teachers like to separate twins at school, but isn't a different school rather extreme? I really think—oh, there's Harry. Harry! Would you come over here, please?"

No, thought Alison. Don't. She watched as Harry, who'd been heading back toward the other kids after grabbing another paper cup—had he taken wine instead of juice?—swiveled toward them and, reluctantly, walked over. He had taken off his tie and unbuttoned the top two buttons of his shirt. He was a year older than Alison, even though they were in the same grade at school, and almost as tall as his father, but thin.

"Professor and Mrs. Shandling," said Rabbi Roth, formally. "My son, Harry. Harry, you already know Alison. But this is her twin, Adam, who goes to a different school. Have you met him?"

"Yes," said Harry. He smiled sweetly at his father and then turned and looked directly at Alison. "I've met the retard *and* his sister."

Feeling oddly detached, Alison watched her mother's face pale and her father's redden. I knew something like this would happen, she thought. And if my mom loses it and screams at Harry, I'll end up paying for it later, at school.

For one glorious moment she didn't care.

And then Rabbi Roth, as pale as Alison's mother, grabbed Harry firmly by the arm and hustled him away.

Gradually, Alison became aware of people around them, a circle of silent, embarrassed stares. "Let's go," said Mrs. Shandling, turning. But she was stopped by a woman standing nearby.

"Please. Don't rush off," said the woman. She was small and plump, with short dark hair and big glasses. She smiled hesitantly, and gestured at a man standing to her left. "My husband, Mike Kravitz. I'm Gloria. We couldn't help but overhear...so sorry..." Her husband nodded.

"We're Betsy and Jake Shandling," said Alison's mother. "These are our children, Alison and Adam."

"The Shandling Sphere, right?" said Mike Kravitz to Professor Shandling. "You invented it?"

Alison's father nodded, cautiously.

"Thought so," said Mike Kravitz. "Saw you on the *Today* show when the Sphere first came out."

Another woman edged her way in next to Mrs. Shandling and took her arm. "About Harry Roth. Not that it's an excuse, you understand, but Margaret Roth died a few years ago. His mother, you know." She lowered her voice. "Cancer."

Several people nodded. "No other children," someone said.

"Well, thank God I haven't got a son like that," said Professor Shandling. He put his hand on Adam's shoulder.

"Uh, yeah," said Mike Kravitz. "Me too." There was an awkward silence, and then he added: "Speaking of those Spheres, I've got one at home. Never could solve the thing. I still pull it out every so often and try."

"I can't believe my daughter goes to school with that boy," Alison's mother was saying to Gloria Kravitz. She turned to Alison. "Is he that obnoxious at school?"

Alison half shrugged, half nodded.

"I used to teach junior high," said Gloria Kravitz. "I know kids, and it's plain to me that boy was just trying to get at his father. You and your family just happened to be here."

You don't know Harry Roth, thought Alison. She glanced over at her father. He had pulled a Sphere from his pocket to demonstrate for Mike Kravitz. Adam was watching, and four or five more people came closer to watch as well.

Alison sighed. It didn't look like they'd be leaving any time soon. She listened to her mother and Gloria Kravitz for a few minutes, and then turned back toward her father.

"And, last, but far from least," the professor was saying, "the Sphere keeps your mind occupied during one of Roth's sermons."

Mike Kravitz laughed.

"I'll pass out a dozen next week," said Alison's father. "It'll keep everyone awake."

A little embarrassed, Alison looked away from her father—and saw Rabbi Roth, standing alone in his robes, without his son, listening to her father make fun of his sermons.

HARRY • April

That afternoon, Rabbi Roth actually asked if Harry wanted to play Scrabble. Of course, this was only after—even more unbelievably—he had suggested Candy Land. "Like we used to," he had said, following Harry into Harry's bedroom. "After all, Shabbat isn't over for a few more hours, is it?"

"I wouldn't know," Harry said. He kept his back to his father. "Religion's your department." He couldn't believe it. Usually his father had the decency to leave him alone.

"Well..."

His father was pitiful. Harry didn't know whether to be angry or disgusted. Couldn't a forty-two-year-old man occupy himself for a few hours? After all, he was the one who insisted on all this Sabbath crap. No car. No electricity. No TV, so

Harry couldn't even watch the playoffs. And now Candy Land. Unbelievable.

"Candy Land," Harry said, "is for six-year-olds." Which was probably about his father's mental age.

"Oh. Well, you always used to like playing it with your mother.... I guess I forgot...."

Forgot what? Harry thought. How old I am? Or that dear sweet old Mom is six feet under?

"How about Scrabble, then?" said the rabbi.

Harry glanced sidelong at his father, wondering why he was being so persistent. That scene this morning at the temple over those Shandling kids? Couldn't be. There'd been worse before. His father never made a big deal; he didn't dare. Harry might refuse to go to synagogue at all. Harry might break the Sabbath and do just as he pleased on Saturdays. On any day. And then what would all the people in his father's congregation think of their rabbi? That was the only thing that worried his father, Harry knew.

Well, they'd see, one day. All of them.

Harry looked at his watch. Three more hours. Then he could get the hell out of the house. Maybe he'd call that girl from school, the one with the tits and the chewing gum and the big crucifix. What was her name?

"You like Scrabble, don't you?" insisted his father.

This was really pretty weird. Harry knew his

father had no more desire to spend the enforced boredom of a Saturday afternoon with his son than Harry had to spend it with him.

"Okay, sure," said Harry casually. "Why not?"

"Great," said the rabbi. "I'll set it up in the kitchen." And he bustled off after the Scrabble board. Harry stared after him, speculating. He wanted something from Harry. Had to be. But what?

And what was that girl's name? Gina. Gina Something. Collarusso.

He'd just love to introduce her to his father.

About halfway through the game, just when Harry had about decided he'd been mistaken, that the old man really only wanted a little fake father-and-son bonding to bolster his ego, his father finally, tentatively, came out with it. "That Shandling family," he said. "I understand the girl is at your school?"

Aha, thought Harry. Now we're getting somewhere. He squinted at the board. It was his turn, but he hadn't put out a word yet, even though the egg timer had almost run out of salt. At the synagogue, his father had marched Harry off in front of everybody. The good father, the good rabbi, ready and able to discipline when necessary. Only Harry knew the truth. His father hadn't said anything. And he wouldn't now, either. He'd back down. Harry would bet on it.

He was really very surprised it had come up again.

The egg timer ran out of salt. Harry had not put out a word.

"Want me to help you?" asked his father.

Harry ignored him. He made the word WAS, building on the W of his father's WOBBLE.

Quickly, his father made the word SERENE, building on the S of WAS. Double word score. The crossword on the board was listing down lopsidedly into one corner. "I, uh, hope you plan to apologize to that girl when you see her at school," he said.

Harry looked his father right in the eye. "Sure," he said. "I plan to tell her exactly how sorry I am." After a couple of seconds, his father looked away.

There was silence. Again, Harry deliberately waited the full three minutes on the egg timer before putting out a word on the board. NO, built on the N from SERENE.

"What," said the rabbi, "uh, what exactly is the problem with her brother? I didn't think he looked retarded...."

Harry looked up from the Scrabble board and watched his father's face as he rambled on.

"I noticed him during services. He was davening...and his face isn't, you know...of course, he didn't talk later, but I thought maybe he was just shy...he can't be retarded." Rabbi Roth was not looking at Harry. "I thought he looked like such a nice boy."

You are too stupid to live, thought Harry. He was suddenly swept by a wave of anger. So that's it, he thought. That's what he's interested in. That boy. That retard. What a joke.

"It's your turn," said Harry.

"Oh." The rabbi looked at the board. Harry's consistent use of little words had severely limited the crossword formulation, so that there were now only a few places that could be used. He frowned. Then he made the word THE, attaching to the E of SERENE, and Harry knew he had given up. The game would be over in another couple of moves.

"Such a nice boy," murmured the rabbi. "It's so sad."

Abruptly, Harry reached over and upended the board. The little wooden letter blocks rained down on the kitchen table. "This game is over," he said.

Harry went to his room, leaving his father to clean up the Scrabble pieces and put them away. He had remembered something, and he went hunting in his closet, where all the old games were, the stuff his mother had bought him when he was little, toys and crap. Harry never used it anymore, but he hadn't gotten around to throwing it all out yet. He found what he was looking for and dug it out.

It was a Shandling Sphere, still in its original packaging, unopened. His father's secretary had bought it for Harry for Hanukkah the year after Harry's mother died.

Harry turned the box over in his hands. Behind

clear shrink-wrap he could see the Sphere, in bright red, blue, and yellow plastic. On the back of the box there was a little ink drawing of Alison Shandling's father, with a blurb.

Harvard physicist Jacob Shandling originally designed the Sphere to help him learn more about his autistic savant son's mathematical abilities. He discovered that Adam can twist the Sphere into one of its three possible geometric forms, in any of the three possible colors, from any starting position! Now, you can test your own skills against Adam's. But be warned: it's tougher than it looks!

Harry headed back to the kitchen, where his father was slowly putting the Scrabble pieces away, and talking aloud. To her. Harry heard: "I know you'd make him do it, Margaret, but I—"

Harry interrupted. "Here you go, Dad," he said, throwing the box hard at his father, who caught it automatically. "Everything you wanted to know about the little retard is on the back." With positive pleasure, he watched his father's face. "Or, as the box says, the little autistic savant."

"Harry—"

"Read it and weep," Harry said, turning. And he thought: And stop talking to her. Just stop, damn it.

• • •

At school that week, Harry deliberately waited until Wednesday, when Alison Shandling had first lunch, like he did, and her friend, de Silva, had third. That meant Alison would be alone. She was a nerd. She didn't have a crowd. She didn't have any friends except Paulina de Silva.

Wednesday was the day Pizza Hut catered lunch. Harry got three slices and hung out by the cashiers, but ten minutes into lunch the traffic had slowed to a crawl and Alison still hadn't come by. He must have missed her. Harry got rid of his tray, stole a new carton of milk, and started to cruise the cafeteria. She couldn't be outside; it was raining. But he didn't see her anywhere.

He spotted Felicia Goren. "You seen Alison Shandling?"

"Don't bother," interrupted Karen McDonough, who was sitting across from Felicia. "She won't do your math homework for you. I asked months ago."

Karen was as stupid as they came. "I don't need help with *not* doing my homework," said Harry. He looked at Felicia, who was flicking her blond hair back with one hand. Felicia laughed.

"She's over there," she said. She pointed to the far end of the very next table. Harry immediately understood why he hadn't spotted Alison himself; he'd been looking for someone sitting alone, and she was at a table filled with kids. But they were seventh-graders, and she wasn't talking with them; she had pushed her tray away and was bent over a book and drinking absently from a big paper cup of soda.

The other kids at her table wouldn't be any trouble.

"What do you want with her?" asked Felicia. Her eyes were avid; she'd been present for the little scene at the synagogue on Saturday. Felicia was a bitch.

Harry smiled. "Business," he said. He walked away, aware that Felicia and her friends were watching, and paused in front of Alison. "Hey, Shandling," he said pleasantly. And then, when she didn't respond immediately, he raised his voice. *"Hey, Shandling!"*

She started up from her book like she'd been shot. But she didn't say anything. She just looked at him like he was an ant.

Harry picked up Alison's abandoned tray, held it suspended in the air over the floor for three slow seconds, and then let it go. It landed with a dull plastic thud. The seventh-graders sitting at Alison's table looked up and stopped talking.

Harry settled himself on the table in front of Alison, one leg swinging. *"Nice* hairstyle," he said, reaching down to touch her hair, caught up in a ponytail by one of those fabric-covered elastic things. She jerked her head away. Harry smiled. "Whatcha reading?" he asked.

"Nothing you'd be interested in," she said. Her

voice was low, barely audible. "And I'd like to get back to it." She looked down at her book again and made to turn a page. Her hand shook just a little.

Quickly, Harry snagged the book, wresting it easily from her. "But I don't want to go away," he said. "I want to find out how to be as smart as you are, Ms. Genius Shandling."

She stared at him. She reached for her soda, but her hand was still shaking and she didn't pick it up, just clenched her fingers around it.

"Maybe," said Harry, "if I read the same books as you, I'll be a genius too. What do you think?" He flipped the book open. *"The Art of Mathematics.* Hey! It's a math book!"

Alison released the cup and made a sudden grab for the book, but Harry held it out of her reach. "Anxious, aren't we?" he said.

"It's my father's," said Alison fiercely. "You give it back."

"Oho," said Harry. He looked up, smiling genially at the kids all around them, who were watching as if this were a circus. "It's *Daddy's* book. Well, well. That explains everything, doesn't it? Genius father gives books to genius child."

Alison grabbed her soda and stood up, turning to walk away. But before she could do more than take a step, Harry slid off the table and moved to block her way. "Hey, what's the rush? Don't you want Daddy's book back after all?"

Trapped, Alison fixed her eyes on Harry's. Then she said, clearly, so that everyone around could hear, "Well, it won't do *you* any good."

"No?" said Harry. He took a step closer to Alison, and she took a counterstep, backward. "Because you think I'm stupid? Well, tell me something then, Ms. Genius. What's with your retard twin brother?" He watched, satisfied, as her eyes flickered. "I'll tell you what I figure. You're freak twins. You got two brains, and he got none."

Harry saw her shock. He watched, satisfied, as even her lips turned white. And for the merest second he had an odd idea—that what he'd said wasn't new to her. That she'd thought of it herself.

Then she raised her cup and flung the remains of the soda in his face.

ALISON • August

"Listen," said Paulina de Silva, "d'you want to go over to the mall this afternoon?"

Alison ate a potato chip. "I don't know," she said doubtfully. "I kind of thought we'd just hang out here. We went to the mall yesterday."

Paulina squirmed on her Adirondack chair. They were in Alison's backyard, eating avocado sandwiches. "I was thinking that I might want that top I tried on," she said. "The red one with the criss-cross straps across the back."

"I thought you said it was the wrong kind of red." Alison tried to be patient. Lately, it seemed that all Paulina wanted to do was go to the mall. Or talk about clothes. They used to talk about real stuff. At least sometimes.

Paulina shrugged. "This morning I realized that

if I got that top, I could wear it with the pants I got last week *and* with a skirt I got last Christmas. And I need new tops." She pulled at the shoulder strap of her bathing suit and looked down at her chest smugly. "Last year's just aren't going to fit."

"I suppose." Alison wondered if she was jealous. Paulina had developed breasts that summer, and Alison had just gotten taller.

"And you'll need new stuff for school, too," said Paulina generously.

"Yeah."

School was the last thing Alison wanted to think about. Never in her life had she been happier than when it finally ended for the summer. The last few weeks of the school year had been unspeakable. She'd done her utmost to avoid Harry Roth, but it seemed as if he'd worked equally hard to be wherever she was. And the whole eighth grade—and a good part of the seventh as well—had been watching. If it hadn't been for Paulina, Alison thought she would have died. As it was, she wasn't sure if she had eaten at all, the last six weeks of school.

In retrospect, though, perhaps the worst had been the scene with her parents. Alison had not told them what was going on. They had enough to worry about all the time, with Adam, and the last thing Alison wanted was to be an additional burden. But Paulina told her own mother, and Mrs. de Silva had turned right around, as Paulina should have known she would, and told Alison's mother.

And Alison had had to beg her parents to let her handle it alone. She had had to cry. And all summer, since, she had been conscious of their eyes, watching her.

It was awful. It was wrong. Adam was the child who worried her parents. Alison was the one who wasn't any trouble.

This was the way it had always worked in their house. Of course, nowadays Adam wasn't as much trouble as he used to be. In the old days, you never knew what would set him off: a balloon popping, a chair that had been moved, some new clothes that he disliked. Sometimes it was nothing at all. And he'd scream and scream and scream, hour after hour. How come it didn't hurt his ears when he screamed like that? It hurt Alison's.

Alternatively, when Adam was happy, it was because of something weird: an electric fan or a digital clock. Years ago he'd spent months fixated on the word "patio," repeating it over and over and laughing that distinctive, high screechy laugh. And he still loved to play with automatic doors, stepping on the area that made them open, and then jumping back, delighted, absorbed, oblivious of other people and their stares.

Alison knew it was awful for her parents. That was why she was important. She was their normal child, their smart child. That was why they loved her so much. And that was why it was so very horrible when Harry Roth caused her, suddenly, to be the focus of their worry. If she worried them she would be a burden like Adam. How could they love her then?

But by now the pressure had eased. School was out and Harry Roth was no longer a daily concern, and also the Shandlings had temporarily stopped going to synagogue on Saturday mornings. The summer services were so small and sparsely attended; it felt awkward, Alison's mother said. So Alison didn't have to watch her parents glaring at Rabbi Roth. Or watch as Rabbi Roth, who never looked at her parents at all, stared at Adam. He'd do this from time to time from his pulpit, whenever the cantor was conducting the service, as if Adam fascinated him. The only thing that could have made matters worse was if Harry had been there. Luckily, though, he'd gone off to camp in New Hampshire for the summer.

Every day Alison thought: if only something would happen to stop Harry from ever coming back.

"So will you come to the mall with me?" Paulina was saying.

"Okay," Alison said. "After Adam comes home from day camp. My mother won't be able to drop us off till then."

"Why not?"

"In case the bus drops him off early or something. Someone has to be here." Alison thought she had explained this before. Why couldn't Paulina remember? It wasn't like Adam was easy to overlook.

Paulina frowned. "We could ask my mother."

"She just had a baby!"

"Four weeks ago," corrected Paulina. She sighed deeply. "Seems like forever."

"Come on. I heard you goo-gooing at him."

"I've stopped, until he starts sleeping through the night. Do you know they expect me to babysit? I mean, I'm a teenager!"

"Right. They should know better than to think you're responsible."

They were laughing when Alison heard her mother call her from the back door. "Alison, could you come in here? *Please?*" Alison stopped laughing. She knew that particular controlled note in her mother's voice.

She went inside, trailed by Paulina. "What's up?" she said. It must be something with Adam, she thought. I haven't done anything.

Mrs. Shandling was pacing the kitchen, an envelope clutched in her hand. "I had planned," she threw over her shoulder to Alison, "to pick out my grad school classes for next term today. Balance the checkbook. Get things in order so I could maybe finally finish my master's degree this year."

This did not look good. "Uh-huh," Alison said. "Well, we can just get out of your way—"

"Read that," snarled Mrs. Shandling, thrusting the envelope at Alison.

"It's addressed to you and Dad—" Alison noticed the return address. Temple Ben Ezra. Her stomach clenched.

"Read it!"

Alison pulled out the letter. She felt Paulina crowding her back, reading over her shoulder.

Dear Dr. and Mrs. Shandling,
We regret to inform you that we are unable to admit your son, Adam, to the fall Hebrew school session. We hope that you will understand. We simply do not have the facilities to address his special educational needs.

We have, however, enrolled Alison in the preconfirmation program, which will meet on Sunday mornings at 10:00.

The letter was signed by Avi Roth, Rabbi, Director of the Religious School.

Alison looked at her mother's livid face. "I'd rather not go either," she said, cautiously. With a part of her mind she was puzzled; somehow she'd gotten the idea that Rabbi Roth was interested in Adam, liked him. But the brunt of her mind was concentrated on her mother. Mrs. Shandling was working up to one of her emotional storms.

"Of course you're not going," Mrs. Shandling said. "After this." She began pacing again. "I have just about had it, do you realize that? I have had it with that man and with everyone like him." She stopped dead again and looked straight at Alison. "I called your father at the lab, but he wasn't there. The bastard."

Alison wasn't sure if her mother meant the rabbi or her father.

"Mrs. Shandling?" Paulina ventured. "Maybe if you sat down?"

Alison's mother whirled on Paulina. "I've called your mother," she said. "She's coming over right now with the baby."

Paulina blinked. "Uh, okay." She exchanged an uneasy glance with Alison.

"Hello? Betsy?" It was Mrs. de Silva, at the front door.

"Kitchen," Alison's mother called to her.

Mrs. de Silva came in. She had baby Marc, head lolling, in the sling in front of her, and was carrying his portable sleeper chair as well as a big bag of baby paraphernalia. "What's up?" she asked. "Betsy, is something wrong?"

Alison watched, in relief, while her mother handed Mrs. de Silva the letter. At least there was another adult here. Mrs. de Silva would be able to calm her mother down. Alison grabbed Paulina's hand and dragged her off to the side. They watched.

"That rabbi knows how good Adam is," Mrs. Shandling was saying, raggedly, to Paulina's mother. "He sees him every Saturday morning. Adam doesn't disturb anybody. He's not disruptive. He's no trouble. It's other people who are the trouble." She had some difficulty getting out the last words.

"Yes, I know, Betsy, honey." Mrs. de Silva put her arms around Alison's mother. But then she stepped back. "Sit down. It's okay." Mrs. de Silva sat down too, facing Alison's mother across the kitchen table.

"I hate them all," Alison's mother said. Her voice was suddenly quiet, calm, controlled. "I hate them. I've had enough of this, I've had enough of this from everyone."

"Yes."

"I feel like every day of my life I have to fight with somebody. Every time I think it's getting easier something else happens. There's some new jerk who needs to be begged or wheedled to help get Adam some service he needs. Or some stupid woman at the supermarket wants to know what's wrong with my son."

"I know," said Mrs. de Silva soothingly. Alison wondered at her calm. Couldn't she see that Alison's mother was nearly out of control?

"And now this," Mrs. Shandling went on. "From

a rabbi. A *rabbi*, Rosalie. He ought to be *ashamed*!" She got up abruptly from the table and paced back and forth, back and forth. "I've had it. I'm going over there, and I'm going to tell that man what I think of him and his synagogue and his religious school." She turned back to Mrs. de Silva. "So if you'd wait here for Adam, I'd appreciate it. His bus comes around two. Alison and I might even be back by then."

What? thought Alison, startled. Me?

"Betsy—" began Mrs. de Silva. But Alison's mother interrupted her.

"Rosalie, I know what you want to say, and I'm sure you're right. But I just don't want to hear it. Why, his son tormented Alison at school all last spring! He's some rabbi, all right."

Alison winced.

"I know," said Paulina's mother.

Mrs. Shandling's mouth tightened. "Alison wouldn't let me interfere. She begged me to stay out of it. She cried."

Hello, thought Alison. I'm here.

"Yes," said Mrs. de Silva.

"That boy is scum."

"Yes, but Betsy—"

"No. I'm going. Where did I put my bag?" Mrs. Shandling looked frantically around the kitchen, finally spotting her enormous handbag on the counter. She snatched it up. "Alison, you can just pull a sundress on over your bathing suit."

"Mom, I really don't want—"

"Go get a dress on. *Now*, Alison."

The leather seats of the Shandlings' Chevy Blazer were dark red and hot. Alison longed for air-conditioning, but her mother seemed to have forgotten about it, and Alison did not want to turn it on herself. She did not want to make any move that might draw her mother's attention to her. Anyway, Temple Ben Ezra was only ten minutes away. Neither Alison nor her mother spoke during the drive.

The parking lot was nearly deserted. Mrs. Shandling pulled into the spot marked SYNAGOGUE PRESIDENT, right next to the old brown Datsun in the spot marked RABBI. Gripping Alison's hand, she pushed open one of the synagogue's heavy double doors and stepped in. The offices were in the small corridor over to the left, behind the main sanctuary. The door to the rabbi's office was open. Her mother marched Alison in.

"May I help you?" A thirtyish woman with dark brown hair was seated behind the desk in the outer office. She was on the telephone, but had placed one hand over the mouthpiece upon seeing them.

Mrs. Shandling ignored her. Still pulling Alison, she walked quickly on into the next office and closed the door. "Rabbi Roth," she said clearly, "you'll remember me. Betsy Shandling. And you should remember my daughter, Alison, too."

"Mrs. Shandling. Of course." Harry's father looked up from the huge old personal computer that, despite its size, was nearly lost amid the stacks of paper on his desk. There were sagging bookshelves hung over the entire wall behind the desk, similarly crammed with books and pamphlets. "Hello. Uh, hello, Alison. Let me just save this...." He gestured at the computer screen, and then fumbled with the keyboard.

"Sit down," said Rabbi Roth finally. "Oh, just a second." He got up to clear more paper and books off the two visitor chairs.

Alison hung back. She watched her mother. Mrs. Shandling waited until the rabbi was through dusting the chairs off and had sat back down. "We won't sit," she said then. She smiled, a thin curl of the lips. "Alison and I have come to ask you about this letter, which arrived today." She handed it to him. "There must have been a mistake. My son, Adam, has been refused admittance to the Hebrew school."

Rabbi Roth turned the letter over in his hands, studying it briefly. "Well," he said. He reached across the desk to hand the letter back to Alison's mother, who folded her arms in front of her, refusing it. After a moment, Rabbi Roth put it down on the desk.

"Mrs. Shandling," he said, "you must understand. We are not equipped for special education.

We haven't the facilities, the experience, the teachers...." He paused, apparently waiting for Alison's mother to say something. When she didn't, he continued: "Much as we'd like to have Adam, we simply can't. We have to think of the other children. There are more of them."

"There are more Christians in the world, too," Mrs. Shandling said. "How would you like it if they said there wasn't room for you?"

"It's been done. Look, Mrs. Shandling—"

"Perhaps we will sit," said Alison's mother, suddenly, dangerously calm again. She nodded at Alison, who perched herself gingerly on the edge of the chair nearest the door. Then she took the other chair for herself. "Go on," she said.

"I really don't know what else there is to say." Rabbi Roth shifted a little in his seat, and then looked directly into Alison's mother's unblinking stare. "I am sorry, Mrs. Shandling."

"Sorry?" said Mrs. Shandling, in her most reasonable tone. "Tell me exactly what you're sorry for, Rabbi Roth. Are you sorry for me because I have a handicapped child? Or are you sorry because you haven't got the—what did you say?—the facilities, the experience, the teachers, that would enable you to allow an autistic boy to sit in a corner of a classroom?"

"Mrs. Shandling—"

Alison's mother ignored him. "You know who

you should be sorry for? You should be sorry for yourself! Rabbis are supposed to be compassionate and understanding, but you...you can't see past bureaucratic details to the simple difference between right and wrong!"

"Mrs. Shandling—"

"It really is that simple, Rabbi. This is a house of God, and you won't admit a Jewish boy because you think it would inconvenience you. Now, I expect this sort of crap from bureaucrats. From strangers. Even from some of my own neighbors. I live with it. But never in my life did I imagine I would see it in a rabbi."

"Please—" Rabbi Roth tried to interrupt. Alison could have told him he had no hope of saying a word. Her mother swept right on.

"But you know what? At least now I don't have to wonder where your son learned right from wrong. Like father, like son. Or don't you know about what Harry was doing to my Alison at school last year?"

Alison winced. For an instant, Rabbi Roth's eyes fell on her. Then they returned to her mother.

"Because the way I see it," Alison's mother had gone on, "it's your son who's handicapped. Not mine. And you know what I wish, Rabbi Roth? I wish your son were even more handicapped. Then you'd be forced to pay attention to your own problems, and you'd have a little more understanding about other people's." Mrs. Shandling paused, and then added, deliberately, "Although, come to think of it, perhaps you don't have the facilities or the experience to do anything about your own problems, either."

She stopped, finally, and Alison dared to take a breath. Rabbi Roth said nothing. He sat unmoving, as if he had magically been transmuted into cement.

"Come on, Alison," said Mrs. Shandling, standing up. "We're through here."

Alison nodded. But at the door, she paused and looked back at Rabbi Roth. He was looking straight at her. Then he looked down.

Alison would have sworn he was going to cry.

HARRY • August

$\mathcal{A}$t the same time that Mrs. Shandling was confronting his father, Harry, at camp, was trying to figure out how he should handle the Rachel Pearl situation. The previous evening had given Rachel the wrong idea.

"There she is," said Mark Titelbaum, nudging Harry. Mark had the upper bunk next to Harry's in Cabin Gimel; the Rachel dare had originated with him.

"Yeah, yeah," said Harry. "I see."

Rachel, in a red two-piece bathing suit and flip-flops, was leaning against a pine tree on the path leading down to the lakefront, holding a towel and pretending not to be watching the upper path.

"Hey, Rach," said Mark as they neared her. He smirked at Harry.

"Oh, hi there," said Rachel. She joined them, falling into step beside Harry, elaborately casual. "Going down for free swim?"

Harry slowed his walk, and so did she. Then he speeded up. So did she. She was smiling brightly.

Great. This was all he needed.

Of course, he wasn't sure if he wanted to discourage her entirely. Rachel Pearl was okay-looking, even with the big teeth, and Harry supposed he wouldn't say no to another "walk" like last night's. There were a lot of ultrareligious kids at this camp, and he'd definitely established that Rachel wasn't one of them.

But it wasn't as if Rachel really liked him. Harry had given her no reason to do so, had barely ever said hello to her before last night, and then only because Mark had told him Rachel had been talking about him. Harry had had to pursue her then, a little. It was expected.

Rachel wasn't hard to figure out; she'd come to camp this year with an agenda. Harry was the fourth boy she'd told her girlfriends she "liked." It wasn't her fault none of them had worked out.

Harry even supposed he wished her luck. He just didn't see himself as part of Harry and Rachel, cute camp couple. Cute fake camp couple, using each other.

Not that he cared about that. It just wasn't worth it. He just didn't want to start anything.

After all, his father would probably be thrilled about Rachel. He'd met Harry's mother at this very camp, all those years ago.

Not that the rabbi talked about that with Harry. Harry wasn't even sure how he knew it. Maybe his mother had told him once. He couldn't remember.

He was tired of camp, anyway. He wouldn't come next year. It would be counselor-in-training year, and Harry had already been taken aside by the camp director. They didn't think Harry was counselor material.

But, Harry knew, they also wouldn't want to offend his father. It would be touchy.

Hypocrites. He would have to think of a nice surprise for the camp director. Just to make sure the rabbi wouldn't be able to pull any strings next year. He wouldn't put it past his father, just to get Harry out of the house.

He wondered, briefly, if his mother would have made him do all this religious crap. Probably. She'd married a rabbi, hadn't she?

Well, that was another thing against her. The list had been building up since she died. No, since she'd gotten sick, and turned into someone else.

"Harry?" Rachel said as they reached the small beach. "I was wondering if maybe you'd want to take out a canoe? Instead of going swimming?"

"Hey, sounds good," Mark sang out. He elbowed Harry. "Let's go!"

"Not you," said Rachel to Mark. She giggled. "Go away." Her giggle was a shrill, witchy heh-heh-heh, and Harry flinched, unexpectedly unnerved by it.

"I'm going to practice diving," he said.

"Why?" said Mark. "I thought you were kicked off the team last week."

"I don't need a team," said Harry, distinctly. He dropped his towel and headed for the water. Rachel scurried along beside him.

"I'll sit on the raft and watch," she said, as they splashed through the shallows. "Okay?"

Harry didn't reply. When the water reached waist level, he dove in and began a rapid crawl to the raft. He didn't wait to see if Rachel could keep up.

The raft was about an eighth of a mile out in the lake, where the water finally became deep enough for real diving. There weren't a lot of campers out there right now; most of them generally stuck to the inner raft area, where the water depth was only about six or seven feet.

Harry had just begun serious diving this year, and he wasn't very good. "Not enough discipline," Pam, the diving coach, had said. He'd fooled around too much, too, which had led, eventually, to Pam kicking him out, for distracting everyone else. Harry didn't really care. He wasn't in it for discipline. He didn't care about developing perfect form. Hell, he wasn't going for the Olympics.

Harry knew exactly why he liked diving. He liked the kick you got in the split second after you dove, before you hit the water. When you knew everything was out of your control, everything already decided, and you could do only one thing: fall.

That was great. Beyond anything.

ALISON • August and September

It was Mrs. Shandling's new friend from the synagogue, Gloria Kravitz, who called and told the Shandlings about Harry's accident.

"Diving," Mrs. Shandling said over Sunday lunch to her husband, Alison, and an inattentive Adam. "A few days ago. Apparently he's in the hospital now. Somewhere in New Hampshire." She flicked a little glance at Alison. "Gloria...uh, Gloria says he broke his back. He won't walk again, she says."

"Well," said the professor, "that might not be true." He also looked at Alison, and then looked away. "Spinal injuries are funny things. I've read stuff lately about new drugs...." He looked at Alison again. He seemed to expect a response.

"Uh-huh," said Alison.

"Jake," Alison's mother said, "Gloria seemed pretty certain Harry wasn't going to recover. Something about the exact spot on his spinal cord that was affected. She said he's lucky that he'll have sensation above the waist."

"Oh," said Alison's father. "I see."

Alison felt the beginnings of a headache. She wished they would stop looking at her. Harry. Paralyzed. She felt numb herself. She tried to collect her thoughts. "When did you say this happened?" she asked.

"I didn't," her mother said. She looked uncomfortable. "Actually, it happened last Wednesday."

Alison began to feel a little sick.

Her father frowned at her mother. "The same day you went to talk to Roth about Adam?"

"Yes."

A sentence swam into Alison's head and attached itself like a barnacle. *I wish your son were even more handicapped.* Her mother had said it that day, in the grip of her righteous wrath.

Alison shuddered.

"Alison."

Alison looked at her mother.

"I've been thinking that I owe you an apology. For that day." Mrs. Shandling waited. Alison was silent. "I shouldn't have taken you with me. But I was so angry I couldn't think straight. I'm sorry. I wish you hadn't seen me like that."

It wasn't the first time, thought Alison, pragmatically.

"Alison? It's just that I was so angry at that man. That excuse for a rabbi." Mrs. Shandling shrugged a little, embarrassed. "I guess I still am. This—Harry's accident—doesn't change that."

"You were mad at Harry, too," Alison said. She stopped, shocked. She wasn't sure where her own comment had come from.

"Well, of course," said Alison's mother. She frowned. "Weren't you? Aren't you still, really?"

"Yes," said Alison. She felt confused. I need to be alone, she thought. I need to think.

"Well," said Mrs. Shandling. She exchanged a glance with her husband. "I was thinking," she said. "Maybe we should talk about Harry. About his accident. I know part of me...well, I know it's awful, but part of me can't help being a little glad." Mrs. Shandling's voice stumbled, and recovered. "I just wondered, Alison, if maybe you'd want to talk about this a little bit."

No, thought Alison. The word shot into her mind like a bullet. She looked at her father.

"You know," said the professor, "Harry probably won't bother you again, when he goes back to school. He'll have other things to think about."

"How do you feel about that?" asked Mrs. Shandling. "Alison?"

Alison stared at her mother.

I wish your son were even more handicapped.

No, thought Alison. The pounding in her forehead picked up in tempo. No. No. No.

"You must feel something," her mother insisted.

Tentatively, carefully, Alison asked, "How do *you* feel about it?"

Mrs. Shandling looked surprised, then relieved. "Well, naturally, it's a terrible thing. He was—is— a nasty boy, and I hated that he was so mean to you. I wanted that to stop. But not this way. But I'm also relieved that we won't have to worry about you anymore."

Good, thought Alison, through the pounding in her head. Don't worry about me.

Alison's father was nodding.

"That's what I think too," said Alison hastily.

She had to get out of there.

"Wow," said Paulina, much later that afternoon. Alison had told her everything. They were at the de Silvas', upstairs in Paulina's room, lying on the double bed and looking up at its canopy. It was a ridiculous bed, with its extravagant pink ruffles and white frills. But Paulina loved it. "You say he'll never walk again?" Paulina continued. "And your mom—"

"It's just that I keep hearing her saying, 'I wish your son were even more handicapped.' And then Harry's accident happening the same day." She didn't mention what she herself had been thinking. She didn't say that she'd been hoping something would happen to keep Harry out of her way.

"Wow," said Paulina again. She was silent for a time, clearly deep in thought. "Chocolate?" she said finally, reaching over and pulling the rewrapped half of a big Cadbury bar from the nightstand. She undid the foil to expose sixteen little squares.

Alison took a square to be polite. "Okay."

They chewed. "So," said Paulina after eating three squares very slowly, "wham. Wheelchair city."

Alison sat up and leaned against the headboard. Paulina stayed flat on her back, one arm flung over her eyes.

"D'you think your mother's a witch?" Paulina asked, conversationally. "D'you think she cursed Harry?"

Alison nearly choked. "Paulina!"

"Just asking," said Paulina. She slanted a look up at Alison. "It's a pretty incredible coincidence, don't you think?"

"Yes. No. I don't know," Alison said. "Look. I guess I'm still just stunned. I mean...well..."

"It's not that I believe in witches and curses and stuff," said Paulina. "But you never know, do you? Maybe your mother doesn't understand her own powers." She sat up. "I saw a movie like that once on TV. This girl got really mad 'cause these other kids ruined her senior prom? She wasn't a witch, exactly, but she had these powers, and then—"

"This isn't a movie, Paulina."

"I know that," said Paulina, with dignity. "Look, I was there too, and your mother was pretty mad. I wouldn't have wanted her cursing me."

"She just gets like that. Especially about Adam." And me, Alison added silently. It was about me, too. "Look, I'm sorry. I don't believe in that magic stuff. It's all just an incredible coincidence."

"Maybe," said Paulina. She leaned forward. "But you know what?"

"What?" Alison said automatically. She thought talking to Paulina had probably been a bad idea. Her head wasn't any clearer. It probably was just a coincidence. And even if her mother...

But Alison's mother wasn't the only one who had wished Harry Roth ill.

"I understand if you don't believe in magic," Paulina was saying. She took another chocolate square and bit off one small corner. "But listen. Do you believe in God?"

"What? Why?"

"Harry deserved it," said Paulina meaningfully. "And Harry got it."

Alison stared at her.

"Divine justice," said Paulina, almost smugly. "You didn't think of that, did you?"

"Actually," said Alison slowly, "I think maybe I did."

"There you go, then." Paulina settled back on her elbows. "I guess the Lord does answer prayers. Makes you feel good, doesn't it?" She reached for some more chocolate.

No, thought Alison, it doesn't. She watched Paulina eat.

She felt very alone.

On the first day of ninth grade, Alison's home-room teacher assigned seating alphabetically. "Roth," Mr. Grandison called, when he reached the fourth desk in the fourth row. "Harold Roth."

Harry didn't swagger to his seat. He didn't mutter, under his breath but loud enough to hear, "That's *Mister* Roth to you," as he'd done the previous year. Instead, there was an uneasy, embarrassed silence. To Alison, the classroom, empty of Harry, was suddenly full of him.

"Harold Roth."

No one moved.

"Does anyone know Harold Roth?" Mr. Grandison persisted.

The silence elongated. Alison looked around the room. One or two of the people Harry used to hang out with were here. Why didn't they say something?

And why didn't Mr. Grandison already know?

What was with this school? Hadn't Rabbi Roth phoned in?

"Well, okay," said Mr. Grandison finally. "I'll find out about Harold. We'll skip his seat for now." He moved to the fifth desk in the row. "Shandling, Alison."

Alison wondered why she wasn't surprised. "Here," she said, moving toward the desk.

Mr. Grandison marked his ledger, frowned. "Alison, I see that you were at the same middle school as Harold Roth last year. Do you know him?"

Alison's stomach lurched a little more. Did she know Harry? What an incredible question. She wet her lips and tried to smile. "Yes," she said finally. "I know him. Not very well, though." That was true, she thought.

"Do you know if he's coming to school this year?" Mr. Grandison persisted.

I don't know, Alison thought. I really don't. "No," she said. "I don't know for sure...." Her voice drifted off.

"Well, Alison," said Mr. Grandison, looking impatient, "you seem to know something about Harold. Why don't you just tell me what it is and I'll check it out."

Alison took a breath, let it out, squared her shoulders, and looked straight at Mr. Grandison. "Harry was in an accident a few weeks ago. He hurt his spine pretty badly, and he's still in the hospital. I don't know when he'll be well enough to come to school." There. She'd said it quite easily after all.

"Oh," said Mr. Grandison. "Well, I'll check into that. How awful." He flushed a little bit. "They should have told me at the office. I don't know why they didn't tell me. Well." He looked at the empty desk, Harry's desk.

"Alison, if Harold Roth isn't attending this year, then of course you'll move up into his seat." He smiled briskly. "We can't have a hole in the middle of the room, can we?" He moved on. "Fifth row, first seat. Shelby, Patricia."

Alison was left staring at the hole in the middle of the classroom.

HARRY • October

"So what happened to you?" asked the teenage boy in the wheelchair. The nurse who had transferred Harry from his own wheelchair to his new bed at University Hospital's rehabilitation ward had just left.

Harry looked up warily. He was tired, and he didn't see how a quick introduction ("Harry, that's your roommate, Paul Zabriskie. Zee, say hi to Harry Roth") meant you were instantly best friends with someone. Or maybe they figured fellow cripples would just hit it off automatically, have a great time.

"What do you care, bozo?" he said.

"Oh, I don't, little boy," drawled Zabriskie. "I just like the sound of my own voice." Paul Zabriskie was a lanky, narrow-shouldered sixteen-year-old with dead-white skin, a shock of thick, straight black hair on his head, and an amazing expanse of beard shadowing his bony jaw, chin, and cheeks. His legs—scarcely more than bones—stuck out of a pair of shorts beneath a Jerry Garcia T-shirt. Harry averted his eyes from them.

"That's good," he said, after a moment, "because I bet no one else does."

"Ooohhh," said Zee. "It's mean." He worked his mouth and spat, expertly, in the direction of the room's sink, twelve feet away. The spittle arced up and then landed in the corner sink with an audible plop. "He sees his chance," said Zee. "He aims. He scores! The crowd goes wild!"

Harry grimaced. If he'd felt better he would've spit right in Zee's face.

"You bring anything to read?" asked Zee, wheeling over next to Harry. "There isn't a lot to do in this place. And they've restricted my TV hours. They say I watch too many soaps."

"Closet," said Harry. "There're comic books in the milk crates." He smiled to himself, sardonically.

"Great," said Zee. He headed for the closet, where nearly every Teenage Mutant Ninja Turtle comic book in existence was stacked in chronological order in two large plastic milk crates.

The collection had been a gift from Harry's father just hours before. In the four weeks since the accident, Rabbi Roth had scoured Boston and

Cambridge looking for back issues. He'd then spent many more hours, when he couldn't be at either the hospital with Harry or at the synagogue, putting the comic books in careful order. He had given them to Harry today, on the occasion of Harry's transfer to the rehabilitation center.

"Whoopee," Harry had said that morning, seeing the milk crates. After examining them for a moment, he had added: "Right. I remember these things. I thought they were really cool—when I was eight. What'd you think—I should read them again now that I'm a mutant too?" Clinically, he'd watched his father pale and turn away. He had hurt his father badly just then. He knew it, and he was glad.

This morning they had attached a catheter drainage bag with tape to Harry's stomach, just above where he'd lost sensation. Harry didn't like it this way. The tape itched. It might be better on his leg where he wouldn't feel it. But would people be able to see it there, bulging through his pants?

He lifted his shirt and looked down cautiously. The bag was getting pretty full. He wished someone would come and change it. He had nightmares about it filling up and bursting, splattering him and God knew who else with urine. Or leaking pungently through his clothes. Or what if the bag was full and didn't burst? What would happen to the pee inside him? Would it back up? Would his bladder explode? No one had said, and Harry couldn't ask.

There had to be information about it on the Internet, or in a book somewhere, but how was he to find it? Even if he went to the hospital's library and used their computers, he wasn't sure he knew how to search properly.

They'd gone on a field trip to the Boston Public Library last year, and the librarian had explained how to use the computers to search for detailed, complex information, the kind you might need for a research paper. There were all kinds of search engines on the Internet, different ones for different kinds of searches. There were also ways to search the library catalogs for books. Of course Harry knew how to find simple things on the Internet, and how to locate a particular book title. But a complicated search like the one he had in mind—where would he even start?

There was another thing Harry needed to know about. But there were mostly women around. Only a few men. And, somehow, it had been only the women who'd asked him if he had any questions. He'd been too embarrassed to tell them what he was worrying about.

And maybe too frightened.

Harry hadn't heard from Rachel Pearl.

He looked at his roommate, who was still occupied with the comic books. Maybe this Zabriskie kid would know. Maybe Harry would get to know him well enough to ask.

Oh, God. A book would be better. A book would be infinitely better than asking.

They lied to you. They lied by omission. They said the library was important for term papers. They never said you might need it for your life.

At night, they attached a bigger bag to the catheter, one that wouldn't fill up so fast, and then they hung it from the bed, right where anyone could see it. It was disgusting. At least the small bag could be kept hidden on his body, under his clothes.

But either way, what girl would ever want to look at it? Rachel Pearl? Harry had to laugh. He wouldn't make it on her short list now. And as for babes like Gina Collarusso, well, forget it.

The bag looked really full now. He touched its plastic side tentatively with a finger and felt the resistance. It needed to be changed. He'd have to push the call button for a nurse. He'd have to ask to have it changed. In front of this Zabriskie kid.

They'd said they'd teach him to take care of himself in this hospital. They said they'd teach him everything he needed to know. Harry hoped it was true.

It was about as much as he dared hope for.

ALISON • November

"Alison," yelled Mrs. Shandling as the phone rang for the fifth time, "could you please get that?"

The words penetrated into the paragraph Alison was reading. She grabbed for her bedroom phone, managing to pick it up midway through the sixth ring.

"Hello?" she said. There was no response. "Is anyone there?"

Finally there came a reply. "Mrs. Shandling? It's Avi Roth. Um, Rabbi Roth."

Harry's father. Alison was astonished. "No, this is Alison," she said finally. "Just a minute, Rabbi Roth. I'll get my mother."

She put down the receiver and went down the hall and into the den, where her mother was working on a paper for one of her psychology classes. "Mom," she said, "it's Rabbi Roth."

Mrs. Shandling turned away from the desk. Alison could tell she was equally surprised. "What does he want?" she asked.

Alison shrugged. "I don't know."

Her mother picked up the extension phone. Unashamedly, Alison lingered, listening in.

"Rabbi Roth. Hello...Oh, no, not at all. I'm, uh, actually I'm glad you called. We've heard about Harry's accident, of course, and we're so very sorry....You got my card, I'm glad....Oh, you're welcome...." There was a long pause while Alison's mother listened. Then she frowned. "Well. I suppose....Right now I'm in the middle of a term paper....If you insist. See you soon, then."

Mrs. Shandling hung up. She swung in her chair to face Alison. "He wants to come over," she said. "To talk."

They stared at each other.

Unable to help herself, Alison went into the family room to peer out the front window and wait for Rabbi Roth. Adam was already there, wearing his favorite rugby shirt and the blue shorts he'd insisted on putting on that morning even though it was really too cold for them. He was sitting on the rug with the earphones on, hands flat on the floor on either side, rocking intensely back and forth.

He ignored Alison. Idly, she picked up the CD case to see what he was listening to: it was an old Rolling Stones, one of her mother's. *Some Girls*.

"Adam still hasn't had lunch," said Mrs. Shandling, wandering in. She knelt down in front of Adam, put her hands on his shoulders to stop him from rocking, and then removed the headphones. "Time to eat lunch," she said.

They went into the kitchen. Alison kept looking out the window. What could Rabbi Roth possibly want?

Ten minutes later she saw his little brown car come slowly up their street. Rabbi Roth parked in front of their house and got out of the car.

"He's here," Alison yelled. She opened the door and watched him come up the walk and steps. "Hi," she said. She stood aside so he could come into the front hall.

"Hi." Rabbi Roth looked as uneasy as Alison felt. He stuck out a hand. "How are you?"

Alison shook hands tentatively. "My mom and Adam are in the kitchen."

"And your father?"

"Uh, at the lab."

"Oh."

Rabbi Roth followed Alison to the kitchen, where he greeted her mother and tried to shake hands with Adam, who was sitting at the table with a cup of milk and a plate that contained three sandwich quarters and a number of orange sections. Adam ignored him.

"Coffee?" said Mrs. Shandling. Alison noted that she had just made a fresh pot. "Is decaffeinated okay? Oh, sit, please."

"Decaffeinated is fine," said Rabbi Roth. He sat down gingerly on one of the chairs in the breakfast nook, across from Adam. Adam did not look up. He put down the sandwich quarter he'd been nibbling and began to form patterns with the food on his plate.

Alison wondered if she should leave. But she wouldn't go unless she was asked. She took a seat as well.

She watched her mother pour coffee into two mugs, put out milk. She watched Rabbi Roth watch Adam, who had now lined the sandwich pieces in a row across the plate, with two orange sections between each pair. He put the extra orange sections down beside the plate. Then he picked one of them up and bit into it, staring at the plate.

Rabbi Roth seemed fascinated.

Finally Mrs. Shandling stopped bustling and sat down next to Adam. "You might want to let the coffee sit for a minute," she advised. "It's pretty hot."

"Thanks. I like it hot." Rabbi Roth sipped.

"Well," said Alison's mother. She looked at Rabbi Roth for a moment, a straight look, carefully neutral. Then she looked at her son. "Take one away, Adam. One of the sandwich pieces."

Adam picked up a sandwich piece from his plate and put it aside, next to the leftover orange slices.

"No, honey. Take it away by eating it. Eat the extra orange slices too. That's how we take them away, remember? Otherwise they have to stay on the plate. And drink some milk. One third. Can you do one third?"

Slowly, Adam began to eat the food that wasn't on his plate. Mrs. Shandling watched him chew, watched until he picked up the milk and began to drink it, and then she turned to Rabbi Roth. "How is Harry doing now?"

"Okay," said Rabbi Roth. "He's been transferred to University Hospital in Boston. They're supposed to have a really good rehab unit."

"I think I've heard of it," said Mrs. Shandling. She took a cautious sip of coffee, made a face, and put the cup down again. "And how are you doing?"

"Okay."

Alison heard the odd note in Rabbi Roth's voice. He's not okay, Alison thought. Of course he's not, but he can't say so.

She suddenly felt very sorry for him.

"Mrs. Shandling," Rabbi Roth was saying, hesitantly, "I didn't come here to talk about Harry. I came to talk about Adam. About his attending Hebrew school at the synagogue."

Oh my God, thought Alison.

Her mother had leaned forward. "Excuse me? You've changed your mind?"

"Well, not exactly. I...that is..." Rabbi Roth paused, and Alison saw him look at Adam.

By creating ever smaller patterns, and eating what he took away to form them, Adam had managed to consume most of his lunch. There was one piece of sandwich left, in the exact center of the plate, with the last orange section sitting diagonally on top of it. Adam was absorbed in watching the plate, his hand hovering over it. He had paid no attention when Rabbi Roth spoke his name, and now he picked up the orange slice, delicately, between two fingers, and bit off half of it. He then returned the other half to the plate, this time upended, one inch to the left of the sandwich.

Mrs. Shandling had noticed Rabbi Roth's fascination. "Adam always eats like that," she commented. "And he never finishes anything completely. We try to make a game out of it, but it can be very frustrating."

Alison wasn't sure, for a moment, if Rabbi Roth had heard. He didn't respond immediately. He was watching Adam separate the bread that formed the sandwich. He put the separated pieces back down on the plate, one to each side of the bit of orange, peanut butter sides up, and cocked his head to one side, considering the effect.

"About Hebrew school," Alison's mother said,

reclaiming Rabbi Roth's attention. "What do you mean, 'Not exactly'?"

Rabbi Roth returned his gaze to Mrs. Shandling. "I still don't see how he could be in class with the others," he said. "But I could tutor Adam privately, if you'd like."

"Excuse me?" said Mrs. Shandling.

"I could tutor Adam myself," Rabbi Roth repeated. He looked toward Adam again, speaking with difficulty. "That day in my office—you were right. I see that now. Or maybe I should say it's been made clear to me....Harry's accident, you know. I've done a lot of thinking. Praying. Trying to understand what happened. What's right. What's just." He looked directly at Betsy again, spread his hands, shrugged a little. "What God wants."

What God wants? thought Alison.

"Excuse me, Rabbi," said Mrs. Shandling. "Am I to understand that you think God wants you to tutor Adam?"

"Well, that's a dramatic way of putting it. But, in essence, yes." Rabbi Roth met Alison's mother's eyes directly. "I know you and your husband are not deeply religious people, Mrs. Shandling. But I believe that things happen for a reason. I might not know the reason, but I believe there is one." Rabbi Roth paused. He drank the end of his coffee and looked over at Adam again.

Rabbi Roth thinks God caused Harry's accident,

Alison thought. On purpose. Because he didn't let Adam into Hebrew school?

The rabbi was continuing, leaning forward, speaking intently. "That day in my office, well, you said some very harsh things to me. About my responsibilities as a rabbi."

And as a father, Alison thought.

Mrs. Shandling cut in. "I was very angry that day, Rabbi. I want to apologize—"

"No, I'm the one who should apologize. You were right, Mrs. Shandling."

Alison saw Rabbi Roth move uneasily in his chair. She wished she could see his expression better.

"Harry's accident was a sign from God," said Harry's father. "A sign that I was wrong about Adam, and you were right."

Her mother was staring at him. "You can't possibly believe—"

"How can I not believe it? It's very clear. Do you know, at first I was just going to call you and apologize. But then I somehow knew it would be insufficient."

Alison's mother had leaned her head in her hands and was rubbing her forehead, slowly, with her fingers. Finally she looked up. "I don't understand. How can you worship God if you think He would hurt Harry just to teach you a lesson?"

Rabbi Roth sighed. "I understand it looks that way to you, Mrs. Shandling. But I have faith that God knows what He's doing."

Alison's mind spun so fast that, for a moment, she couldn't understand a single thought in it.

"I don't know what to tell you, Rabbi," Alison's mother said. "Honestly, I don't."

"Tell me that I can tutor Adam. Twice a week, maybe, one-hour sessions? We could start by learning some prayers. Does Adam like to sing? Adam?" Adam didn't look up, but his hands on the bread stilled, and Alison could tell by the stiffening of his shoulders that he knew he was being addressed. "Can you sing, Adam?"

Adam didn't answer. After a moment, he began moving the pieces of bread around on his plate again.

"He can hum," said Mrs. Shandling. "He likes music. He does that rhythmic rocking, you know. To music."

"Rock," said Adam suddenly, softly. "Rolling Stones." He didn't look up from his plate.

"He likes the Stones," Mrs. Shandling agreed. "And the old Motown music, you know." She smiled a little. "Probably not what you had in mind?"

"Well," the rabbi said, "I could try. And Adam likes being in synagogue. I've noticed that."

"Ah." After another moment, Alison's mother sighed, exhaling. "I just don't know, Rabbi. You're offering a lot more than I had in mind, to be honest. In a class, well, Adam could just sit there. He might or might not take something in. I was willing to risk it."

"Were you willing to risk it with regular school?"

Mrs. Shandling shook her head. "You're right, of course. Adam goes to a special school. Which brings up another problem. Have you ever dealt with an autistic child, Rabbi? Do you have any idea what you're getting into?"

"I could learn."

"Maybe," said Mrs. Shandling. She looked doubtful. "I just don't know."

"At least think about it. Please."

"It's not just my decision, you know. I'd have to talk it over with my husband."

"Of course."

"Even if we said yes, you should have the right to change your mind. After a session or two, you might decide it's not working out."

"I suppose that's possible. But I would like to try, Mrs. Shandling. It would mean a lot to me. And possibly to Adam."

"I'll think about it."

"Thank you, Mrs. Shandling," said Rabbi Roth. "I appreciate it." He looked at his watch, and rose. "Well. I'd better be off. They keep strict visiting hours at the rehab unit."

"I'll see you out," said Mrs. Shandling. "Adam, say good-bye to Rabbi Roth."

Rabbi Roth waited. Nothing. "Good-bye, Adam," he said finally. "I hope to see you soon."

He reached across the table and, very gently, took Adam's hand from where it rested beside the plate. He shook it and put it back down. "Good-bye. And good-bye, Alison."

Alison nodded back. She watched Rabbi Roth and her mother leave the kitchen.

Rabbi Roth thought Harry's accident had happened because God wanted Rabbi Roth to know he'd made the wrong decision about letting Adam go to Hebrew school.

Alison had wondered, herself, if God was punishing Harry for persecuting her. That had been an awful enough thought. But, in it, at least Harry had actually done the thing he was being punished for.

Rabbi Roth thought Harry was being punished not for his own actions, but for his father's.

It was a far more awful idea.

Alison wondered if Harry knew what his father thought.

HARRY • November

$\mathcal{H}$arry was in his chair in the rec room, practicing lifts and watching *1010 Brookside* on television. At first, he'd sneered at his roommate when Zee turned on the afternoon soap opera, but he'd been watching it with Zee most days for nearly three weeks now, and it was pretty interesting after all. There were some gorgeous babes. Right now Anna, who was some kind of secret agent, was on a stakeout. Something to do with drugs. Anna had a gun, an accent, and a lot of long dark hair that hung over one side of her face. Zee preferred Cecilia, but Harry couldn't see it.

Buzz.

His watch alarm was set so low that only Harry could hear it. Automatically, he tightened his hands on the armrests and lifted his body, shifting his buttocks slightly on the chair's cushion. Lift

up, over, down, release. It took only a couple of seconds, and you'd have to watch closely to see that
he was doing it. Harry knew that for sure because
he'd watched himself in the mirror at the gym.

"Hey," he said to Zee, "move your ass."

"Yeah, yeah." Zee grimaced and did, ostentatiously. "Happy, little boy?"

"You want to get sores like Doherty, that's your
business," said Harry, offended. "It's your ass."

"You'd better believe it," said Zee.

Harry turned his attention back to the soap,
where some guy was sneaking up on Anna from
behind. Zee wasn't too regular about his lifts,
Harry had noticed. He'd only been trying to help.
Well, he wouldn't again. He watched Anna get hit
on the head and slump to the ground. So much for
her gun.

Buzz. Harry did a lift: up, over, down, release.
He had a sudden vision of Doherty's pressure
sores, and did a second lift, just for luck.

Eileen Costas, the physical therapist, had made
Harry and Zee look at Doherty's sores. Doherty
had been flat on his stomach at the time, hospital
gown parted so they could see his buttocks. Harry
had only just managed to keep from throwing up.

First of all, he'd been embarrassed and humili-
ated for Doherty. He was a grown-up. How did he
feel, lying there, helpless, exposed, a lesson in
what not to do? How could Eileen do that to him?
How could Doherty let her?

And then there were the sores themselves. Okay, Doherty was a quad, and couldn't use his arms for shifting. Still, though, he should have done something. It was his responsibility. Doherty had even said so himself when Eileen got through lecturing. He'd gotten careless. Eileen said he'd take months to heal, and that was if he was lucky. If not, he'd need surgery. And what if it happened again?

Harry didn't plan to get pressure sores. He didn't plan to have his ass look like that—or be on public display if it did. He had set his watch alarm to go off every five minutes during the day. After a week, Harry figured the shifting would be automatic. If it wasn't, well, he'd go back on the alarm until it was. And then he'd find some way to contend with regular turning in bed at night. By himself.

"What a great idea!" Eileen had said about the watch alarm that morning, had said loudly, enthusiastically. Eileen was always loud and, when she wasn't issuing dire warnings, enthusiastic. Somehow she had found out what Harry was doing. He really didn't know why people couldn't just mind their own business.

But, since the accident, he'd found that people had absolutely no concept of what was and wasn't their business. Take Eileen. She was supposed to do what she was paid for, tell him about pressure sores, exercises, stuff like that. He understood that. And he needed her. He understood that too, even if he didn't like it. But when they were working in the gym, why did she have to answer his questions in such a loud voice? Why did she have to tell other people what he was doing, how he was doing, why he was doing? Why was his body suddenly everybody's business? Why was Doherty's? And even if it was, even if they really did have to know (and he didn't see why all of them had to know everything), then why were they all so determined to make sure he knew they knew?

Harry sighed. *1010 Brookside* was almost over. Anna had been tied up and carried off. It was a funny thing. He felt like Anna. Someone had snuck up behind him and hit him over the head, and now he was tied up, a helpless prisoner. Buzz. A prisoner who had to do lifts. He did one.

A prisoner who had to go and see Dr. Jefferies. Dr. Jefferies was a psychiatrist. Harry had to see her twice a week. Dr. Jefferies was even worse than Eileen. At first she had been useful, had answered many of his questions without his even needing to ask them, had even given him two or three books that'd been kind of helpful.

But lately she'd been trying to get into his head.

Harry wheeled himself out of the rec room and down the ward corridor. He stopped for a second at the nurses' station to let them know where he was going—as if he didn't do the same thing every Tuesday and Friday!—and then pressed the button for the elevator. His watch buzzed while he waited. He did his lift.

"Good job, Harry!" he heard one of the nurses call. "Keep up the lifts!"

Harry winced. He didn't reply, he didn't turn. How could they tell? They shouldn't be able to. He would practice more with the mirror.

At last the elevator arrived. He wheeled in. There was a couple inside, wearing street clothes. They were blocking the buttons.

"Press seven, please," Harry said. He occupied himself in wheeling around so he was facing forward. Maybe he should have rolled in backward. He'd forgotten about that.

"Sure," said the man, a little too heartily. Harry could feel his eyes. Looking at the crippled kid. Looking away from the crippled kid. Looking again.

Asshole.

The couple got off on six. An orderly with a patient in a wheelchair—a patient who didn't really need one, Harry noted—got on.

Seven. Harry wheeled out and followed the green painted line on the floor down a couple of corridors and into the next wing, to Dr. Jefferies's office. The door was open. Good. At least he could get the appointment over with on time. Sometimes the previous appointment ran over a little and Harry had to wait. Harry's own appointment never ran over. He watched the clock to make sure of it.

He sighed. He went in.

"Hi, Harry," said Dr. Jefferies. She was a tallish,

thinnish woman with brown eyes and thick gray-brown hair worn in a messy bun. There were age spots on her hands. She had on an oversize white cardigan with big wooden buttons down the front and the name tag KARIN JEFFERIES, M.D. pinned slightly askew on the sweater near her collarbone.

Harry nodded. He wheeled himself to his usual corner, next to the old wooden chair with frayed orange cushions that Dr. Jefferies always sat in. He'd been very surprised by that, at their first meeting. He'd thought she'd sit behind her desk. He had said so, and she had wanted to talk about that for the longest time. But she still sat in the orange chair.

She sat there now, pulling it a little closer to his than he would have liked. Not that he would say anything. He knew better now.

"How are you today, Harry? How are things on the ward?"

"Fine."

"Have you got anything special you'd like to talk about today? Or ask?"

"No."

There was silence. It stretched for a full minute before Dr. Jefferies spoke. "Well, Harry. Tell me a little bit about your mother."

"My mother?" said Harry, suspiciously. "Why? We never talked about her before. Anyway, she's dead. Didn't you know she's dead?"

Dr. Jefferies nodded. "Uterine cancer, wasn't it?"

Harry didn't reply.

"When did she die?" Dr. Jefferies asked.

"Over four years ago," Harry said, after a pause. He had to answer. It did no good when you didn't answer Dr. Jefferies. She just kept right on. It was exhausting.

"You were eleven? Is that right?"

After another pause, Harry said, "Yes. Well, no. I was almost eleven. It was right before my birthday.

"How close before your birthday?"

He shouldn't have said anything. "The day before."

"Your mother died the day before your birthday?"

"Yes." For no reason, he added: "September twenty-seventh."

"Ah," said Dr. Jefferies. She looked thoughtful. "Then her funeral would have been the very next day, the twenty-eighth, on your birthday. Is that right? Harry?"

"Yes," said Harry. It had had to be. His father had said so. It was what Jews did. The funeral had to be right away, within twenty-four hours. Unless it was the Sabbath. You didn't bury anyone on the Sabbath. On your son's birthday, yes, but not on the Sabbath.

"Ah," said Dr. Jefferies again. "Do you remember the funeral, Harry?"

"No," said Harry. He wasn't going to tell her about that.

Dr. Jefferies nodded. It was impossible to tell whether she knew he was lying. "What was your mother's name?" she asked, tapping her pencil against her hand. She did that, played with a pencil. She never wrote anything down, at least not while Harry was there. He worried sometimes about whether she did later, whether there was a file somewhere, on her computer maybe, that was full of his personal business. If he wasn't careful, pretty soon they'd have enough information on him in this place to start a library.

"Margaret," he said.

"Do you remember what she looked like?"

"I have a picture."

"Do you remember her yourself?"

Sometimes, he thought. Sometimes when I'm about to fall asleep at night. If I don't try too hard. And that time at the supermarket, when I called, when that woman turned around, if it had really been her I would have known. I would have recognized her. I would have remembered what she looked like.

But there were many Margarets to remember. The laughing one, before she got sick. Then the thin, tired one who held him too tightly and scared him with her talk of death. And then, finally, the one his father still talked to when he thought no one was listening.

That one was not his mother. That one belonged only to his father. He hated that one.

Dr. Jefferies had been silent, watching Harry's face. He knew she was waiting for him to answer. He knew he couldn't. He looked away from her. He looked down at his hands, at where they lay on his lap, on top of his useless legs. They're ugly hands, he thought. Ugly legs.

"Does your father ever talk to you about your mother?" Dr. Jefferies asked.

Harry looked at his watch. There were eons left of the fifty minutes. He looked at his hands again. He didn't care what she did. He wouldn't answer.

Dr. Jefferies was tapping the pencil again, silently. "Your father never talks about your mother with you, does he?"

He wouldn't answer.

"Nod if that's right, Harry. Just nod."

After a minute, Harry nodded.

"Do you know why he doesn't, Harry? Just shake your head yes or no. Do you know why he never talks about her with you?"

Yes, Harry thought. He doesn't need to talk to me. He talks to her. He stared at Dr. Jefferies. He said nothing.

"Do you ever wish he would? Even once?"

Harry swallowed. He kept his eyes on his hands. They were fists. Finally he nodded.

"Have you ever asked him anything about her, Harry?"

He shook his head. No.

"Why not? Did you think that he didn't want to talk about her?"

A nod. Yes.

"You didn't talk about her because your father didn't want to talk about her?"

Yes.

"Do you know why he didn't?"

No.

"Do you talk with anyone about your mother?"

No.

"Does your father?"

Harry shrugged. He doubted it. He tried to take a deep breath. To relax his shoulders. His hands hurt from being clenched. He flexed his fingers.

"You don't know?"

"No," said Harry aloud. His voice sounded creaky. He cleared his throat. "No," he said again. That was better. He wasn't going to cry. He looked up at Dr. Jefferies. She was watching him steadily. He looked down again. He wasn't going to cry. She had enough in her files about him.

"Did you love your mother, Harry?"

All the air left Harry's lungs. He felt like Dr. Jefferies had just punched him in the stomach. He stared at her, speechless.

"You loved her, didn't you?"

He stared. If he kept his eyes wide he wouldn't cry.

"I know you did. Nod if I'm right. Just nod."

Harry looked down at his hands, but they were around his arms now, clutching tight. He hugged himself harder. He blinked rapidly.

"Just nod."

If he could only get out of here. He closed his eyes. Please, he thought. Leave me alone. I thought we were supposed to talk about my legs. Let's talk about that. Let's talk about how I'll never walk again. Hell. Let's really go for it. Let's talk about weird sex for cripples. Let's talk about how I'll never have a girlfriend, a life. Never get away from home. From him.

"Just nod."

Harry nodded. He wasn't even sure what he was agreeing to.

Dr. Jefferies sighed. She leaned forward a little, toward Harry. "And you miss her, Harry?"

He nodded again. That was what she wanted. And he couldn't explain. How could he explain that it was more complicated than that? She'd think he was a monster. He'd never get rid of her.

Dr. Jefferies sat back. There was silence. Harry concentrated. He hadn't really let go; there'd been only a few tears. He accepted a tissue from Dr. Jefferies, but he wouldn't look at her. He breathed.

For minutes he sat there. Finally he tried his voice. "I'd like to leave now," he said. He didn't look at Dr. Jefferies.

"We have some more time," said Dr. Jefferies.

Her voice was soft. "I'd like to talk more about your mother and what you remember."

"Well, I wouldn't," snapped Harry. He could feel himself getting angry. He raised his head and glared at Dr. Jefferies. She was looking at him thoughtfully. There was another silence.

"Okay," she said finally. "Another time, then." She got up. "Look. I need to run an errand in another part of the hospital. Why don't you stay here until you feel comfortable about leaving? I haven't got another appointment here for an hour. Okay?"

"Yeah," said Harry. It came out in a whisper. He waited for her to leave.

"By the way, Harry," said Dr. Jefferies suddenly, pausing in the doorway.

He looked up, in her direction but not directly at her.

"I noticed, during this whole session, you did lifts regularly. Even when things got rough. That's great."

Harry's eyes focused on her for an instant. He was suddenly indignant, shocked out of his misery. It wasn't her business...how had she noticed ...the mirror...

But it was true. His watch had beeped, he'd done the lift, every five minutes throughout the session. He hadn't thought about it at all. It had been automatic.

ALISON • December

On a Sunday two weeks after Rabbi Roth had first proposed that he tutor Adam privately in Hebrew, Alison found herself with her mother and Adam in the Chevy van, about to be dropped off with Adam at Rabbi Roth's—and Harry's—house. "Adam won't be comfortable there alone, not at first," her mother had said to Rabbi Roth. "And he's used to being dropped off places with his sister."

Alison didn't mind. She had a Tolkien book with her. More, she had to admit to a certain curiosity. She wanted to see Harry's house.

At first, her father had been incredulous when his wife explained that Rabbi Roth thought God wanted him to tutor Adam. "The man is insane," he had said, flatly. "I'm not going to let a religious maniac near my son."

Mrs. Shandling had disagreed. "Jake, he's just

distressed. He realizes he was wrong, and this is his way of making amends."

They had argued for over a week. At one point they had even asked Alison's opinion, but she had evaded them. And finally they had compromised: one or two sessions, just to see how it went. "Roth will give up fast," Alison's father had predicted. "He has no idea what it's like. What if Adam has a tantrum? I'd just like to see him try to cope." Listening, watching, Alison had thought that her father almost wanted Rabbi Roth to fail with Adam.

Petersboro Road, where the Roths lived, was in a fifties-era development of tiny, look-alike capes built on lots scarcely big enough to hold them. It was a far cry from the street on which the Shandlings lived, with its half-acre lots, new, self-consciously varied houses, three-car garages, and pools. It made Alison uncomfortable. They had so much, thanks to her father's Sphere. And this neighborhood was only ten minutes by car from theirs.

They pulled up in front of number fifty-three, a gray house with nothing to distinguish it from its fellows except its color. "I'll be back to get you in an hour," Mrs. Shandling told Alison.

Alison nodded. "Come on, Adam," she said. She opened her car door and got out, glancing up the walk toward the front door. Rabbi Roth had opened the door of his house and was standing just outside on the front steps, waiting for them. He waved.

"Adam?" said Alison. He hadn't moved from the

backseat. For a moment she thought he would simply refuse to get out, but then, without looking at Alison, he did, slamming the car door behind him.

Alison could feel her mother's concern. "Maybe I should come in too," Mrs. Shandling began. "After all—"

"We'll be fine," Alison cut in. She didn't want her mother with them. And it wasn't like it used to be, when Adam refused to go anywhere new, even if one of them was with him. She took Adam's hand. "Come on."

Adam pulled his hand away. But he came with her, up the walk. On the top step, Alison turned and waved to her mother. Then they went in. After a moment, Alison heard the sound of the car driving away.

Rabbi Roth ushered them into the living room. Alison looked around. Adam stood on one foot and fixed his eyes on the other. Alison hoped he would not take it into his head to begin spinning around and around. Sometimes Adam would do that. He never seemed to get dizzy.

"Well," Rabbi Roth said. "Alison. Adam. Welcome." He smiled at them uncertainly.

Alison smiled back. "Hello," she said.

Adam said nothing. He put down his foot. Then he raised it again and stamped it down hard. And then again.

Uh-oh, thought Alison. Quickly, loudly, she said, "Orange juice." She looked at Rabbi Roth.

Adam had paused in his stamping.

"Orange juice?" repeated Rabbi Roth.

"One half," said Alison firmly, just as loudly.

It worked. Adam giggled. "One half," he shout-ed. "One half!"

Rabbi Roth looked bewildered. "I think I do have orange juice," he said, as if it were unusual. "In the kitchen." He gestured.

"Fine," said Alison. "Thank you." She followed Rabbi Roth into the kitchen, Adam trailing her.

Rabbi Roth poured juice into two glasses. Alison took hers. "Adam?" Rabbi Roth said, holding the other glass out to him.

"One half," said Adam. He giggled. He kept his hands behind his back.

"Half a glass," said Alison to Rabbi Roth, patiently. "It's a one-half day for Adam."

"Oh," said Rabbi Roth, uncomprehendingly. He looked at Alison and then at the full glass, as if uncertain what to do with the extra orange juice. Finally, he poured half the glass back into the orange juice carton. Then, tentatively, he held it out to Adam.

Adam took it, without looking directly at Rabbi Roth. He examined the juice closely, sniffing at it for an entire minute. Then he drank half of it.

"One half!" he repeated. He held out the one-quarter-filled glass again to Rabbi Roth. Rabbi Roth took it.

"He'll do that no matter how much you pour

in," explained Alison, sipping at her own juice. "Because today's a one-half day."

"Uh-huh," said Rabbi Roth. He put down the orange juice glass. "Well," he said.

Alison felt a little sorry for him. Her father was right. Rabbi Roth didn't really know what he was doing. He probably didn't even realize what a nasty little scene Alison had just averted.

She wondered if she should tell the rabbi that on a one-half day, Adam might try to do exactly one half of everything he was told to do. Like go halfway into a room. It could be pretty annoying. She opened her mouth, but the rabbi spoke first.

"Make yourself at home anywhere, Alison. Adam and I will be in the study." He held out his hand, carefully, to Adam, who looked at it but did not take it. "The study is down the hall. Why don't you just follow me there, Adam?" Rabbi Roth started away, slowly. Adam looked at his sister.

"I'll be here, Adam," said Alison. "You can follow the rabbi. He's going to teach you some Hebrew, remember?" Good word, "follow," she thought.

"One half," said Adam.

"You can't do one half of follow," said Alison. Adam thought about that. Alison hoped that Rabbi Roth would take her hint; it was all in what you said. She watched Adam turn and go down the hall, slowly, after Rabbi Roth, hopping on one foot after the other. The one-half walk. They went into the room at the end, and Rabbi Roth closed the door partway behind them. After a minute, Alison could hear his voice talking to Adam, but not what he was saying.

She sighed, relaxing a little and looking around. So this was where Harry lived. It really was a small house. Here in the kitchen, for example, there was barely enough room to walk around the table. How would Harry manage in a wheelchair? And what about the front steps? Wouldn't they need a ramp?

She had better go and read. Alison put her empty juice glass down in the sink, hesitating a second before washing it and Adam's glass out carefully and placing them in the dish drainer. Then she walked back to the living room and sat down on the couch. Too much furniture in here, too, she thought, for a wheelchair. And the carpet should go. She opened her book.

Alison wasn't exactly enjoying *The Two Towers*. Right now Frodo, the Ringbearer, was day by awful day inching closer to the Dark Lord's tower. He hoped to elude capture and destroy the Ring. But the Ring was evil and it was replacing Frodo's will bit by bit with its own.

The Ring was stronger than Frodo. And Frodo knew it.

It was too terrifying. Alison dog-eared her page and closed the book. She looked at her watch.

There was half an hour before her mother came back. And it sounded like the lesson was going well. She could hear the murmuring from the study. Rabbi Roth's voice, singing. She recognized the melody of the *Sh'ma*.

Harry's father. A rabbi.

What was he doing here with her brother? Shouldn't he be with Harry?

How was Harry, anyway? Weeks and weeks, and no one had said. At school it was like Harry had never existed.

Alison thought of him every day.

She wondered where his room was. It had to be one of those two closed doors in the hall. Maybe she'd just peek in at the nearest door.

It was Harry's room. She stepped just inside the threshold, poised on the balls of her feet, one hand behind her on the knob.

It was small, maybe ten by twelve feet, but extremely neat. The furniture was all dark wood. The twin bed was meticulously made with a blue and beige bedspread, the nightstand next to it was bare except for a red windup alarm clock that had stopped and a lamp with a blue shade. The dresser across from the bed had an empty goldfish bowl on it. A white rag rug had been laid beside the bed. The closet was closed. A small three-shelf bookcase was full, but, unlike Alison's larger one at home, not stuffed.

The rest of the small house wasn't neat at all. There were piles of things—books, newspapers, and just plain junk—everywhere. But this room was very tidy. Did that mean Harry was neat?

Alison could still hear the voices from the study. Adam's now, for a second, singing a little. She stepped fully into Harry's room, closing the door behind her. She knew she shouldn't be doing this. She opened the closet and peeked in. Clothes were hung on a double-tier rack to the left. Shelves had been built in on the right. There were games there and toys. She noticed a big, worn, stuffed tiger. You belong on the bed, Alison thought. She closed the closet and went over to the bookcase. Her mother always said you could tell people by their books. Harry had a lot of comic books. Alison didn't know much about comic books, though Paulina liked the love ones. He had a lot of books about sports. And he had a few novels. A well-worn copy of *The Three Musketeers*. That was a good book; Alison had read it. And there was J.R.R. Tolkien's *The Hobbit*. It, too, looked read.

Alison touched the book's spine. She wondered if Harry had read the sequels, the trilogy she was reading right now. Maybe he had also thought that Frodo didn't have a chance. Maybe that was why he was always so mean. Maybe he thought evil always won.

She wondered if that was right. Paulina would

have said that good won when Harry had the accident, but Alison knew that wasn't true.

She went over to the nightstand and pulled its single drawer open. It was empty except for a picture frame, turned facedown. She reached in and turned it over. It was a woman's face, a young, pretty woman with dark hair drawn back from her forehead, and brown eyes with thick, definite eyebrows. Harry's eyes.

Harry's mother. Suddenly, Alison felt terrible. She had no business here. She replaced the picture carefully and closed the drawer. She had better leave before she was caught.

She returned to the living room. It was noon now. Soon her mother would come. And she could go home, have lunch, and then go over to Paulina's.

But it really did sound like the rabbi's lesson with Adam was going well. And, if so, she'd be back here next week. Back in Harry's house.

HARRY • February

$\mathcal{O}$nly one more session with Dr. Jefferies, Harry thought between dribbles, and that's it. Thank God. Balancing the basketball in his hands, he sighted carefully and shot. Too low again, damn it. He wheeled himself in pursuit of the ball, which was slowly bouncing, and then rolling, off to the side. He grimaced. He wouldn't have had anything to do with this stupid little half-size court if Zee hadn't been such a maniac about one-on-one. Or if there was anything else decent to do in this place.

But Zee had already left, and today was Harry's own last day in the hospital. His father would come to get him tomorrow morning, and after that, while he'd be returning on an outpatient basis for physical therapy with Eileen, he wouldn't have to see Dr. Jefferies. Insurance didn't cover psychotherapy after a certain number of sessions, and when his father had asked him if he wanted to continue anyway ("It'll be difficult to afford it, but if you think it would be helpful, then of course..."), Harry had said no. He meant it too. He had just barely managed to keep Dr. Jefferies from getting too deeply into the topic of his mother, and then she had started in on his father, and Harry's "relationship" with him. Unbelievable, that woman. Really.

Today would end it.

Retrieving the ball, Harry hesitated, grimacing. He still had forty minutes to kill before he had to go see Eileen, and then, after her, Dr. Jefferies. He could go on practicing foul shots—and chasing the ball all over creation after every one—or he could practice dribbling. He'd gotten better at maneuvering the chair with one hand while dribbling with the other. His father had paid for a special chair that was supposed to be okay for sports. Of course it was pretty pointless without Zee there to guard against.

What we mutants really need, thought Harry bitterly, is computer gaming. He got off another shot quickly, almost without aiming, and watched it teeter, miraculously, on the rim before dropping triumphantly outside the hoop and bouncing away again. Computer gaming, he thought again, starting after the ball. A nice game you play without needing your body—or another human being—at all. Just perfect.

· · ·

Harry arrived at Dr. Jefferies's office one minute early for his appointment, but her door was open and she was inside, at her desk, writing on a notepad. Something about me? Harry wondered. The desk, unusually, was covered with stuff: stacks of computer paper, files, books.

From the doorway, he watched her for a few seconds, until she looked up and saw him. She smiled and gestured him in, putting aside her notepad but keeping the pencil as usual, getting up and going to close the door and pull up the ugly orange-cushioned chair so that she could sit down near him. She seemed glad to see him, but Harry knew it was just her job. And also she liked prying into his business. Probably everybody's business. She liked knowing things so that she could know them and maybe so that she could write them down somewhere, like on that yellow pad of hers that she had just put away. You owned things you wrote down.

"Do you write things about me?" he asked, abruptly. He knew she'd be surprised; he never started a conversation with her. But today was the last day. He didn't have to be quite so careful.

"Why do you ask, Harry?"

"You do, don't you? Or you wouldn't have asked why I asked. I knew it. I knew it all the time." He glared at her.

"It makes you angry."

"No kidding," Harry drawled out, mocking her.

"What makes you think it makes me angry? What makes you think I feel that way?" There. Those were the sorts of things she said all the time. He stared at the wall over her shoulder. There was a little rug hung up there, fringed, red and white with a little bit of green and yellow. What was a rug doing on the wall? Did she think it was pretty? Well, it wasn't. It was stupid.

Dr. Jefferies was leaning forward. "Harry. I think it makes you angry because you feel violated. Do you know what that means? Like you've been invaded, trampled. Is that how you feel? Harry?"

"You bitch," said Harry.

There was a silence. Harry looked at the rug.

If she knew how it felt when she...*violated* people, then why did she do it? Why did they all do it?

"You're angry," said Dr. Jefferies. "I can understand that."

Harry wanted to call her something worse. Many worse things. He controlled himself. It was the last day. If he could just hold on...

"I'm sorry, Harry," said Dr. Jefferies. "Let me explain to you about writing things down. First, yes, you're right, I do keep notes about you. About everyone I see. It's so that I'll remember what we talked about."

Harry stared at her. Then slowly, deliberately, he looked away.

"But my notes are just for me," Dr. Jefferies

continued. "Anything that happens between a doctor and a patient is confidential. It's illegal for anyone else to see my notes.

"Anyway, I wouldn't want to show them to anyone else, Harry. The way I see it, it isn't wrong for me to write things down, but it would be wrong if anyone but me saw what I wrote."

Harry thought about that. He wasn't convinced. "Someone else might see them anyway," he said.

"Not if I can help it."

"Why?" said Harry instantly, suspicious. "What's in them?"

Dr. Jefferies laughed. "Nothing awful. You know why, Harry? Because you're not so bad." She laughed again, shaking her head. Looking at him as if she liked him.

What did she mean? Of course he was awful. Everyone thought so. She ought to think so. He had just called her a bitch, after all. When he had called Mrs. Thompson a bitch last year at school, she had turned purple. And it was only one word; if he wanted, he could say a lot more. He always knew just how to hurt people. Like Alison Shandling at school, last year. Like his father.

Dr. Jefferies was tapping that pencil on her hand again, inches from his knee. He grabbed it and broke it in half, hurling the pieces across the room. They collided with the wall behind Dr. Jefferies's desk and fell feebly to the floor.

"Harry..." Dr. Jefferies began.

Harry ignored her. He wheeled himself closer to the desk. He swept out with his arms, knocking the paper stacks and files and books to the floor. He grabbed the notepad that Dr. Jefferies had been writing on when he'd come in and looked at it.

Melissa may have been abused, he read. *The burn marks on her feet are typical—*

"Give me that," said Dr. Jefferies. "Right now."

Somehow, Harry managed to look away from the words blurring on the notepad.

"Harry."

Still not looking at Dr. Jefferies, Harry reached the notepad in her direction and felt her take it.

There was a pause. Harry looked at the stuff he'd knocked to the floor. Dr. Jefferies looked at him. He closed his eyes. He wondered who Melissa was. He wondered how old she was. He wondered what she thought of her life.

"Harry," said Dr. Jefferies. Unexpectedly, her voice was gentle. "Suppose I promised you that I won't keep notes for a while, until you say it's okay."

Harry opened his eyes. He looked at her. What was she talking about? "It doesn't matter what you promise," he said. "Today's the last time I'm seeing you. I go home tomorrow."

"I'd like to go on seeing you. Once a week, maybe, on a day that you come here anyway to see

Eileen for physical therapy. I spoke with your father about it, and he said it was okay with him if it's okay with you."

"It's not okay with me." Weakly, he added: "I really don't like you."

"Well, I do like you."

"No, you don't. You're always poking into what isn't your business. Pretending it's your job, pretending you like me—"

"I'm not pretending anything." Dr. Jefferies sighed. "Look. You don't have to make a final decision now about coming back. I'll talk to you about it again, maybe in a couple of days when you come for your next appointment with Eileen."

"I won't change my mind," Harry said defiantly.

"Maybe not," said Dr. Jefferies. "But I hope you will. And remember—no notes. I promise."

"Yeah, right," said Harry.

His last appointment with Dr. Jefferies. Ha. He should have known she wouldn't let him off the hook that easily.

Why was it that he felt—just the tiniest bit—relieved?

ALISON • February

Alison awoke very early the Sunday after Harry came home from the hospital. She and Adam were due at the rabbi's at eleven o'clock that morning for Adam's lesson, and this time Harry would be there. It would be the first time Alison had seen him since the accident.

Would she have to talk to him? Would he want to talk to her?

She lay curled up in bed, on her side facing the wall, one hand cupped beneath her cheek, eyes open, thinking, afraid. It was still nearly completely dark outside her quilt, but with that strange dark gray light that came before dawn. Alison wished she could stay in bed, wrapped in flannel and wool, forever.

Down by her foot she could feel something large

and soft and lumpy. Josephine, who had somehow slipped down there during the night. She reached under the covers and pulled the old, stuffed cotton crab up into her arms. Josephine was in bad shape—faded from red to a mottled pink, stuffing escaping from a seam, an antenna missing—but Alison loved her and had kept her through last month's purge, when she had packed up all of her other stuffed animals for charity. "Maybe I'll keep Josephine," she had told her mother, who had looked on for a few minutes from the doorway while Alison ruthlessly threw her childhood into a single cardboard box. "As a bed decoration. I don't really need her anymore. I'm too old for that. I'm going to be fifteen this year, you know."

"I do know," Mrs. Shandling had said. "Listen, Alison, is it okay if I keep Victoria?" She fished down in the box for a small porcelain doll dressed in nineteenth-century period costume. "I'm a little more sentimental than you are."

"Sure, Mom," Alison had answered, tolerantly. "Whatever you want."

It was true, Alison thought, hugging Josephine to her chest, that she was too old for stuffed animals. But sometimes, like last night, well, it didn't do any harm, did it? And no one needed to know.

Alison rested her chin on top of her crab. With her index finger, she pushed in some of the leaky stuffing. Josephine had always been special. Not everybody liked crabs, but Alison felt there was something trustworthy and secure about them. Okay, so they were a little alien. But a crab would keep secrets. When she was little, and believed that all the dolls and stuffed animals came alive at night when the rest of the house slept, Alison had known that her own secrets, no matter how horrible, were safe with Josephine. Josephine would never tell Adam's toys—which Adam never played with, but kept perfectly lined up on a shelf in his room—that sometimes Alison hated her brother.

And now, even though she was a teenager and practically grown up, Alison still felt safe with Josephine.

There was a little more light in the room, enough to see the clock. Six. Alison got out of bed and went barefoot over to the window, bringing Josephine. It had snowed the night before, lightly blanketing the grass and the pool cover in the backyard. There wasn't enough snow to force a cancellation of Adam's lesson with Rabbi Roth. Alison knew her father would have the driveway and the car swept clean in only a few minutes.

Maybe, since they had to go, she could bring something with her for Harry. As a peace offering. Even if Harry didn't know what her mother had said or what his own father had thought, it might make Alison feel better. Not that there was any guarantee Harry would accept a gift.

She wondered if he had changed. She wondered how it felt, to know you'd never walk again.

And what about sex? Was Harry's penis paralyzed too? Would Harry be like one of the eunuchs in the days of the Ottoman Empire, who could be trusted to guard the harem of beautiful women because they couldn't make love? Alison had thought of asking her mother these things, but hadn't dared. And Paulina wouldn't know any more than Alison. Anyway, she didn't like to talk to Paulina about Harry. Paulina didn't understand why Alison cared.

Alison herself didn't quite understand.

Maybe she would look it up at the library. She could do a computer search to find the right books. Why not? She wanted to know.

She turned back into the room, switched on her bedside light, and climbed back into bed. She considered the books piled on her nightstand. Then she reached for one.

She could always forget herself in a book.

In the end Alison brought the Tolkien books with her for Harry. Maybe he had already read them, maybe not. It wouldn't be too conspicuous a present, anyway, since they weren't new.

She kept all three of them stacked on her lap in the backseat of the car as her father drove to Harry's house. She hadn't needed to come. At breakfast, after her father polished off the last bit of maple syrup from his plate with a pancake and picked up the magazine section of the Sunday *New York Times*, he had looked directly at Alison and said, "Harry's home now. So if you don't want to go with Adam today, I will. I'll bring the crossword and do it there." He opened the magazine to expose the crossword and waved it at Alison as if he thought she'd never seen it before. "I never get to do the crossword. Your mother always grabs it first and does it in ink."

"So buy another paper," said Mrs. Shandling, lunging across the table to try to grab the magazine away from her husband, who held it out of her reach. But both of them were watching Alison.

Next to Alison, Adam was floating pancake pieces in a sea of maple syrup, using a fork to navigate them in an ordered circle around the rim of his plate, totally absorbed. When they were very small, when Adam was simply Adam and not her brother with whom something was wrong, Alison had played games like this with him, giggling hysterically whenever he did. She wondered briefly if Adam had missed her when she stopped playing. He'd never seemed to. He was the same whether she was there in spirit, or just in body.

"No, it's okay, I'll go," she'd answered her father. She had dealt calmly with her parents' are-you-sures, because suddenly she *was* sure. She felt the way she'd felt when she was in elementary school, and the other kids made fun of Adam. She'd realized then she had to defend him, and herself. Walking away would only make it worse.

She didn't look back as she got out of the car with Adam. Adam was used to coming to the Roths' now. He went right up the unswept walk, up the new wooden ramp, leaving sneaker prints in the thin snow for Alison to follow. Rabbi Roth was at the door. He always was. Alison figured he must watch for them. Well, for Adam.

"Good to see you," he said. Alison noticed that his blue flannel shirt was misbuttoned, and that his shirttail wasn't completely tucked in at the back of his pants.

"Hi," she replied. Adam didn't say anything. Alison looked around. The living room was different, emptier. The coffee table was gone, and the newspaper piles had been cleared away. The rug was still there, though, and it had wheel tracks on it. The wall-to-wall carpet had too deep a pile. It ought to go completely, Alison thought.

The room was also empty of Harry. Somehow she'd expected him to be right there in the living room when she came in, sitting in his wheelchair, ready to spit malice. Ready to attack first.

She followed the rabbi and Adam into the kitchen for a glass of the orange juice that, ritualistically, Adam always drank before they went off to the study. Also no Harry.

He's in his bedroom, Alison thought. He's hiding from me. She was suddenly certain of it. Why? It wasn't like him. He wouldn't be afraid of Alison. Of a bunch of kids, maybe, but not of Alison alone.

Had he seen any other kids yet? Alison would be scared of that, if she were him.

"Well, Adam and I are off," Rabbi Roth was saying to her. "Have a seat somewhere. I see you have books to read. That's good."

Alison nodded. She always had a book. The rabbi seemed even more awkward with her than usual. She decided to be direct. "Where's Harry?" she asked. "I'd like to say hi."

The rabbi blinked. Stuttered. "Uh. In his room. Resting. I didn't want him to disturb you."

You're worried about *me* being disturbed? thought Alison. Not him? "It's okay," she said aloud, just as she had to her parents earlier. She drained her orange juice and placed the glass carefully in the sink before turning to smile at him. "You go on. I know Adam's anxious to get started. I'll just go say hi to Harry." She slipped past the rabbi, feeling his astonishment and his anxiety, but ignoring it. He was an easy person to ignore. She went down the hall to Harry's bedroom door. It was an inch ajar.

So. He'd been listening. Now *that* was like him. Yes. Smiling grimly to herself, Alison knocked. Then some instinct she hadn't known she possessed took over. Without waiting for an answer, she pushed the door all the way open, and looked unwaveringly into Harry's astonished eyes. "Hi," she said.

He wasn't in his wheelchair. He was sitting on the edge of the bed, still in pajamas, with the wheelchair—the folding kind—next to him. Possibly he'd just propelled himself out of the chair and onto the bed. His hair was a mess, way too long, and uncombed. But aside from that he didn't look too bad. Just pale. Taller, if you could say that about someone sitting down. His cheekbones stuck out, and his nose, and they hadn't the last time Alison had seen him. Last June. More than eight months ago.

He recovered quickly from the shock of her intrusion, from her unaccustomed aggression. "Shandling," he snarled. "Didn't anyone ever teach you to wait for an invitation? I suppose you'd barge right in on someone taking a piss, too." He glared, just as Alison had thought he would.

"No," said Alison. She was amazed at her coolness. She stepped into the room and closed the door behind her, still holding the three paperback books. She leaned against the door, looking at Harry. Let his father wonder what was going on. He wouldn't interfere, not unless she and Harry started shouting. And he had to stay with Adam, anyway. "So," she said to Harry. "So." And then suddenly her sangfroid fled. She couldn't remember any of the things she'd planned to say. She kept her face blank. Her mind whirled.

"So," Harry mimicked. "So what the hell are you doing here?"

Alison found her voice. "I came with my brother."

"I meant what the hell are you doing in my bedroom. I can't believe you're supposed to be so fucking smart. Are you sure you're not brain-damaged like your brother? Huh?"

I am smart enough to handle this, Alison thought. It's the same old routine, isn't it? But it was hard to remember that she sympathized with Harry. That maybe she owed him.

He was looking at her now, taking stock of her as she had of him. She was abruptly conscious of how the ponytail she wore exposed her face, of the stiffness of her new, leggier, jeans, and of her breasts beneath her sweater, cupped by a bra she hadn't needed last year.

"I wanted to see if you were still a complete jerk," she said finally, quietly. "I don't know why I had any doubts."

"Well, there's nothing different about me," Harry said. His eyes narrowed. "I still hate your guts, you spoiled little rich bitch. Think you're so smart. Think you're better than everybody else."

Alison felt all the air leave her lungs.

"So get out of my face," Harry finished, his voice

barely a whisper. "I've had enough. Get out of my room. Get out of my fucking *life*."

Alison's eyes were drawn to his legs as if mesmerized by them. They looked ordinary enough, thin in the maroon pajama bottoms, bare white feet sticking out at the ends.

She could not look away.

"I said get the fuck out of my life!" Harry repeated. "*Leave me alone*." If he hadn't been whispering, it would have been a scream.

Alison managed to force her eyes up his body, to his face, as white as his feet. She looked into his eyes. She thought he was about to lose it, and begin screaming at her.

Her head, miraculously, cleared.

She reached behind her with one hand for the doorknob. "I can't leave you alone," she said. The words came from somewhere deep inside her, and she knew, however horrible, they were true. "And I won't." With her other hand, like a child throwing food to a lion at the zoo, she tossed the books she'd brought for Harry onto his bed beside him.

Then she opened the door, turned, and fled.

HARRY • March

For the next two Saturdays, Harry flatly refused to go to Sabbath services at the synagogue. He didn't plan to go ever again.

His father couldn't make him. "What?" Harry had said the first time. "You're going to push me screaming in the wheelchair?" His father had stared at him. Then he had left the room and, a little later, walked off to the synagogue without Harry.

And for the first time in his life, Harry had spent Saturday morning watching TV.

His father kept asking, though. This morning, he had sat right down with Harry in the kitchen and taken the sports page away from him and told him that he really wanted him to come. He understood how Harry's faith might be wavering, but it was important to keep up the form of things. That was what life was about. And he could assure

Harry that everyone at the synagogue really wanted to see him. They asked about him all the time. They were concerned.

"Yeah, I bet," said Harry.

Finally his father had begged. He had even offered to take the car. God would understand, he'd said. It was in the Talmud that you could make allowances for sickness, and—

"I'm not going," Harry had interrupted. "And that's final." He had wheeled himself out of the kitchen.

His father had left without him. In a few more weeks, Harry figured, even his father would get the idea. But, to help him along, he kept the TV on, even after his father got home.

Later that afternoon, when the Celtics game broke for commercials, Harry pressed the remote. Bowling. Click. A documentary about heart disease. Click. Blonde on Home Shopping Club in a suede suit. Back to the game, but they were advertising Bud Dry. Click click click.

Well. Sports, of course, but besides that it looked as if he hadn't been missing much all these years of no TV on Saturday. Not that that was the point. He clicked back to the game. The commercials had to end sometime.

Maybe if they had cable. He'd never ask, though. He wasn't going to ask for a damn thing.

He wondered if his father knew he had the TV on. The door to Harry's bedroom was closed. He clicked up the volume.

Okay, third period. Boston had the ball. Pass. Score. 76–54. It wasn't much of a game. Maybe he'd switch to bowling.

He clicked up the volume again.

Nothing.

He had to get out of the house. Over two weeks, and he'd gone out only for his appointments with Eileen and Dr. Jefferies.

He almost thought he missed the rehab.

No, he didn't. He just wasn't sleeping too well. But he wouldn't take those pills. There was no way.

He had school on Monday. Dr. Jefferies had prodded him about it both times he'd seen her. Hey, change of pace. Nice to know she had other interests besides his mother's death and his relationship with his father.

And, of course, tomorrow was Sunday. Time for round three with Alison Shandling.

The books she'd brought that first time, week before last, were over there stacked on top of his bookcase. Harry hadn't read them. He had told her what to do with them last week, when she'd barged in for the second time.

At least she'd waited for his reply to her knock before entering. She just hadn't paid any attention to it. She'd walked in, looked straight at him, closed the door. This time he'd been dressed, and in his chair. He'd been ready. He'd suspected she might pull something again.

"Hi," she'd said. She had a couple of Diet Coke cans and a bag of potato chips that she must have brought with her because his father sure hadn't bought them, and, of course, she had a book, tucked under one arm. "Catch." She threw a Coke underhand.

Harry had caught it, but not because she knew how to aim. If he'd missed, he thought, she would have picked it up and tried to hand it to him. He put it down on the floor next to his chair. "Get out of here," he said, really quite pleasantly.

"I hope you like barbecued potato chips. They're my favorite." Alison was pulling out the desk chair, reversing it next to the desk so that it faced him, and sitting down, placing her Coke and book on the desk and starting to open the chips. She had a little trouble. It was a large bag, and she kept her head down while she pulled at it. Her fingers slipped on the package. And suddenly Harry knew she was scared, the way he'd always known that sort of thing about other kids. He could smell it.

It calmed him. This was his room. This was his house. "Why don't you give it to me?" he said.

She looked up.

"I'll open it. My arms work." Harry watched while she got up slowly, took a half step forward, and reached out and over to hand the bag to him, keeping herself well away. Yes. Definitely scared, he thought. Even physically scared.

His chair was now nearer the door than she was. He wondered if she'd noticed.

He smiled at her.

He ripped open the potato chips. Then, putting the bag down in his lap, he wheeled his chair closer to her, moving it right in front of the door. Their knees were almost touching. She couldn't get out now until he let her, not unless she were to push him out of the way, and she would never do that. That was another thing he always knew, what another kid would or wouldn't do in a fight. He held out the bag.

Harry saw Alison's eyes flicker to the door, but they lingered only a moment. She didn't crack too easily, but he could still sort of see what she was feeling underneath. That was one reason she had made a good target for him the year before; she was someone he could hurt but who wouldn't cry and attract attention and who didn't have a lot of friends.

Uncertainly, Alison took the bag. "Don't you want some?" she said.

Harry decided to wait and say nothing. He'd sit there, blocking the door, silent. She'd get more and more scared. Finally, when she couldn't stand it anymore, she'd make some excuse, say she had to leave. Get up. Fumble with her book and the chips and the Coke. And then she'd have to ask him to get out of her way.

Harry smiled. He looked at her, but Alison shifted her eyes away before it could develop into a staring contest. "Well," she said. She reached into the bag, took out a large chip, and bit into it. A few crumbs dribbled down onto her blue and gray sweater, onto her breasts. Deliberately, Harry looked at them and let his eyes stay there a long moment. He looked at her face just to check. Yes, she was turning red. She was reaching, awkwardly, to brush off the crumbs and then pausing, not sure what to do about them. She'd last three minutes, tops.

He felt good.

Then she spoke. She wouldn't meet his eyes. "I'll just read. Paulina and I hang out and read a lot. It's a good way to keep company when you don't want to talk."

They hung out together and *read*?

Harry watched, incredulous, as Alison put the potato chips down on the desk, the bag's open end toward her. He noticed that her hand was shaking a little, but she leaned right back in the chair, crossed her legs, and opened her book somewhere near the middle.

Of course she wasn't really going to read. It was just her way of trying to outface him. She was a little tougher than he'd thought.

And a lot weirder.

Alison turned a page of her book. *The Caine Mutiny*. She was definitely faking it, though.

A minute passed. Two.

Alison turned another page. Slumped back a bit more. Then she reached into the potato chip bag with her left hand and extracted a large chip. She put it in her mouth whole. More crumbs dribbled down on her chest, but this time she ignored them.

She turned another page, paused, and then went back, eyes scanning the previous page. Then she nodded and flipped ahead again.

She ate some more chips. She turned another page.

And then another.

She'd forgotten Harry was there.

He reached over and grabbed the book, pulling at it. She looked up, startled, but held on. "Hey! Let go!" She looked right into his eyes this time, furious. "Get your own book!"

It was the last thing he'd expected her to say. Harry was so surprised, he let go. Alison glared at him. "I brought you some books last week," she said. "This one's mine."

She was *insane*. What did she think this was, Book-of-the-Month Club? Unexpectedly, Harry wanted to laugh.

She had settled back in the chair, clutching her precious book to her chest. "You can't read it like that," Harry said, before he remembered that he wasn't going to talk.

"I'm not stupid," said Alison.

Oh, well. He might as well talk; his strategy

hadn't worked anyway. "I don't want your books," Harry said. "I hate to read. You can just take them home and shove them."

Alison blinked. "You hate to read?"

"Yes."

"But you have books. Over there. You have *The Hobbit*. That's why I brought you the other Tolkien books. Didn't you read it?" Her voice was curious, nothing more.

"No," said Harry again. "Why should I?"

She looked bewildered. "You don't like to read?" she repeated, as if she thought he had to be lying.

"No! Why should I? You act like reading is fucking breathing or something."

"I never thought about it like that." She frowned. "I guess I never thought about it at all. I just assumed...no, not even that. It just didn't cross my mind. Breathing. Well, maybe. For me." What the hell was she talking about? She was looking at him. "You really don't read even for fun?"

He wasn't going to tell her what he'd been reading about the last few months. It hadn't been fun, that was for sure.

"Only nerds read. You read all the time; that makes you Queen Nerd."

"Queen Nerd," said Alison thoughtfully. She grinned. "I know I'm supposed to be insulted, but it sounds kind of Egyptian. King Tut. Queen Nerd. Kind of nice. But I thought I was a nerd because I'm lousy at sports?"

"Doesn't help." Queen Nerd sounded *kind of nice?*

"Oh," said Alison. "I get it. A fatal combination of things." She nodded.

Harry was curious. He couldn't help himself. "Don't you mind being a nerd?"

"Yes," said Alison, honestly. "But you know, I don't think I'll mind now that I can think of it as being Queen Nerd. And I couldn't give up reading, not even to be as popular as Felicia Goren. It wouldn't be worth it." She took a handful of potato chips and held out the bag to Harry. "Are you sure you don't want any? They're good."

Harry stared at her. He took a handful. He spent the next ten minutes listening to Alison tell him what had happened so far in *The Caine Mutiny*, and then his father knocked. Adam's lesson was over, and Mrs. Shandling was here to get them.

"Well, 'bye," said Alison. She picked up her book. "Do you want the chips?"

"No," said Harry, moving his chair out of her way.

"Okay, I'll take them. See you next week."

He recovered himself. "Don't bother, Queen Nerd," he said.

She had laughed. Really laughed. "See ya."

She had meant it, Harry thought, remembering. She'd liked being called Queen Nerd.

What an odd girl she was.

ALISON • March

Alison was up by eight the next Sunday, which wasn't unusual, but she was also showered and dressed. Alison never got dressed before she had to. But she was supposed to go and see Paulina before she and Adam went to the Roths' at eleven.

Paulina had called the night before, late, after Adam had gone to bed and literally seconds after Rabbi Roth had called. Alison had had trouble listening to Paulina because she'd been wondering what Rabbi Roth's phone call had been about. What if Rabbi Roth had said something to her parents about Alison talking to Harry? They'd be horrified. They thought Alison just kept out of Harry's way. But she hadn't been able to hear what her mother was saying because Paulina was jabbering on, something about the mall and Felicia Goren.

She had finally interrupted Paulina. "Look," she had said. "I can't talk now. What if I come over tomorrow morning?" They had agreed on eight-thirty, and hung up. Then Alison had wandered down the hall and lingered outside the den, where her parents were talking.

"Well, do you think a bar mitzvah would be possible for Adam?" her mother was saying.

A bar mitzvah for Adam? Alison was amazed. She listened even more intently.

"Roth really thinks Adam can do it?" her father asked.

"That's what he said. Jake, he really sounded excited. I've never heard him sound so enthusiastic."

"Adam's fourteen," her father said. "But that really doesn't matter....Well." His voice strengthened. "Why not? If Adam's willing. I did it, after all."

"Do you think Alison will mind?" her mother asked. "Rabbi Roth didn't mention her. But she could have a bat mitzvah. I can ask her."

No, thought Alison, alarmed. Thank you, but no. She'd been to bar and bat mitzvahs. She didn't want to stand up in synagogue and go through the whole, lengthy performance, chanting in Hebrew, being formally initiated into adulthood. She didn't even like *going* to synagogue.

And she wasn't at all sure about God.

"Well, if she wants to," her father was saying. "Of course. But it might be nice to have Adam do this all by himself." He paused. "Betsy?"

"Yes?"

"Have you noticed, Harry Roth doesn't come to Sabbath services anymore? It's no wonder Roth's enthused about Adam. I almost feel sorry for him. Roth, I mean."

"Me too," Alison's mother had said. "And, Jake…"

Alison had slipped away, feeling strange. Once in bed, it had taken her ages to fall asleep. There was so much to think about: her parents, Adam and this bar mitzvah thing, Rabbi Roth.

Harry. Her parents didn't understand at all, did they? Why would Harry want to be a good son to Rabbi Roth? Rabbi Roth couldn't even let Harry's accident be about Harry. It had to be about Rabbi Roth and his relationship with God.

By contrast, it was a relief to wonder what Paulina wanted to talk about. It wouldn't be anything heavy. Probably just some gossip. Paulina was a terrible gossip.

Adam was in the kitchen eating Raisin Bran. Alison hesitated, but she didn't really feel hungry. "Adam," she said, "I'm going to bike over to Paulina's, just for an hour or so. Will you tell Mom and Dad?"

Adam regarded her stolidly.

"Well?" said Alison.

"Alison Shandling, you're dressed," said Adam, in his unmodulated, slightly too loud voice. He looked upset. Adam didn't like it when things were different from usual.

"Yes," she said. "I needed to be dressed to go visit Paulina. I can't go in a nightgown, can I?" She kept her voice calm.

Adam giggled. Alison breathed a sigh of relief. "You can't go in a nightgown!" he said.

Alison nodded. "Inappropriate."

"Inappropriate," agreed Adam. Alison knew it was a word he'd heard as often as his own name. He was still giggling softly, but he nodded when she reminded him to tell their parents where she was, and when she'd be back.

Alison put on her jacket and gloves and headed out. She got her bike from the shed and began pedaling down the mostly empty streets. It was cold, and she biked fast, to stay warm. It was funny, she thought. Adam had calmed down so quickly. Maybe he really could have a bar mitzvah. He was in so much better control now.

But Adam was still autistic, still himself. Alison knew that would never change.

Arriving at Paulina's, she parked her bike in the driveway and approached the back door cautiously. It was very early. But Paulina had remembered, though she was still in her nightgown, and she was waiting to let Alison in. Together, they went through the kitchen and down the hall toward Paulina's room.

Mrs. de Silva was standing in the doorway of the baby's room, cradling him in her arms, and humming. She was wearing a robe, and looked sleepy. "Hi, Alison," she said. "Paulina, I don't suppose you girls could watch Marc for an hour or so, so your father and I could sleep in?"

Paulina looked rebellious. "Mom," she started.

Alison interrupted. "Sure," she said. She took the baby from Mrs. de Silva before Paulina could stop her. He'd gotten so big. "We can still talk, Paulina. He's not crying or anything. We'll put him on the bed. Or I'll hold him."

"Oh, all right. But if he was your brother—"

"Thank you, Alison," said Mrs. de Silva. Paulina shut up. Alison thought that she would love a brother like Marc, a soft, cuddly, curious little bundle that grabbed and pulled at your fingers and nose and settled right into your arms as if he belonged there. She rubbed her cheek against his head.

"You should see him throw up," said Paulina cynically. They had entered her room. She threw herself onto her bed and then sat up and moved over into the corner, leaning against the bedpost, to make room for Alison. "Or change his diapers. Disgusting."

"He's so sweet right now, though." Alison put Marc on the bed and climbed into the other corner against the wall before picking him back up.

Paulina snorted. "Let's see how long it lasts. But listen, I didn't want to talk to you about babies. Something amazing happened. You'll die."

"What?" Alison freed her hair from Marc's fist. She should have put it in a ponytail.

"It's just incredible."

"What?"

"Well, I was at the mall yesterday, you know, just looking, and guess what? I ran into Felicia Goren." Paulina leaned forward, her words tumbling out in a stream of excitement. "First of all, she talked to me. I mean, she was really nice, it was amazing. And guess what? She says Jason Shepherd *likes* you." Paulina paused for dramatic effect. "Well? Could you die? I can't stand it, I'm so jealous."

"Felicia's making it up," Alison said automatically. What? Jason Shepherd was a friend of Harry's. Or he used to be. Or they were on some team together, she forgot. But Jason was really popular. Not like Harry. Jason had curly black hair and thick eyebrows that nearly met over his blue eyes, and he played sports but he wasn't entirely dumb. He sat behind Alison in math. Sometimes he would talk to her about the homework. But he had never had anything else to say to her. "I thought he was going out with Cindy Pasquale."

"They broke up two weeks ago. Don't you know anything? And Felicia says he wants to ask you out. He asked George Montesano to ask her to ask me to ask you if you'd go. She says she couldn't believe it either. But it's *true*. Swear to God." Paulina delivered all of this in one breath.

"But I've never gone out with anyone." Alison searched her memory. No. Jason Shepherd hadn't said anything much to her lately. And she was a nerd; Harry had just told her about how that worked. This couldn't be true.

"I know that! Neither have I. But we have to start sometime, right? And Jason *Shepherd*."

Alison listened to Paulina burble on about how popular Jason was, and how maybe they would be popular now too, because, look, Felicia never even used to talk to Paulina, and she'd been so friendly yesterday, and wasn't it exciting? "But we're nerds, Paulina," she finally broke in. And I'm Queen Nerd, she thought. "I just don't get it. Those kids don't like us. Jason Shepherd barely speaks to me. Listen, maybe Felicia is playing some horrible joke, and they're all going to be laughing at us. Felicia's mean, you know she is."

"So what? She's popular."

Alison tightened her arms around Marc, who let out a squawk in protest. "I can't believe you just said that." She loosened her grip. "Sorry, baby," she murmured. She looked up and met Paulina's eyes. After a minute Paulina's fell.

"I know," she said. "But I get really tired of being a nerd."

"Me too. But we won't always be. My mother says that in college—"

"That's years away!" Paulina wailed. "I want a boyfriend now!"

They stared starkly at each other. Marc had settled down again. He was sucking wetly on two fingers, watching his sister from beneath his incredible lashes. Alison rubbed his head with her chin. "It's just that I don't believe it," she told Paulina finally.

"Don't you *want* it to be true?"

Alison blinked. "I don't know. I...I guess." Did she? She wasn't sure. At least when you were Queen Nerd, you knew what was what. You knew who your friends were, and you knew who they weren't.

But she hadn't known how Paulina felt until now.

"It might be true," said Paulina. "You know you've gotten pretty lately." Her voice held a slight tinge of accusation. "Even my dad said something."

Alison shrugged. She felt embarrassed. "That's stupid. I mean, he's grown up."

Impatient, Paulina rolled her eyes. "What are you going to *do*? I have to call Felicia and tell her."

"I don't know."

"You can't say that! You have to say yes so I can tell Felicia so she'll tell George so he can tell Jason!"

Alison looked down. She played with Marc's fingers for a long time. Finally, not meeting Paulina's eyes, she shook her head. "Tell Felicia," she said slowly, "to tell George to tell Jason that he has to ask me himself."

"Alison!" Paulina was horrified. "He'll never do it. Not unless he knows you'll say yes."

"Too bad." Alison felt cold.

"You're going to ruin our only chance! We'll be nerds forever. And I'll never have a boyfriend."

This isn't about you, Paulina de Silva, Alison thought. Then she was shocked at herself. Quickly, she explained. "Listen. This way, if it is a joke, we won't be made fools of. And if it isn't, Jason will ask me out himself."

"It doesn't work that way! You'll lose him!"

Alison stared at Paulina defiantly. "I don't care." And she thought, Why should I care? I don't know him. I can't like someone I don't know. And I won't come running just because he's cute and popular. If he doesn't ask me out, that's fine. Things will stay the same. Paulina and I will stay the same. Being Queen Nerd isn't so bad.

Alison stood up. "I have to get back," she said. "Adam and I have to go to the Roths' for Adam's lesson." And I have to see Harry, she thought. He'll know if Jason and his friends are making fun of me. And he'll tell me. He won't care if my feelings are hurt. He couldn't care less about my feelings.

He won't play any games. It was a comforting thought. She bounced the baby one last time before handing him to Paulina.

"Okay," said Paulina reluctantly. She trailed Alison down the hall and through the kitchen. "Listen, think about it some more. Okay? Call me this afternoon. I won't call Felicia till after. Please?"

"Okay," Alison promised. She knew she wouldn't change her mind. "I'll call you."

"Good."

Frowning, Alison pedaled home.

HARRY • April

$\mathcal{J}$f not for Alison Shandling, Harry thought he might have died that first week back at school. It was pretty funny, being grateful to Queen Nerd. Not that she knew about it, of course.

Each day began with the utter humiliation of getting dropped off by his father. The whole process was intolerable: the handicapped parking space that his father pulled into; the endless minutes while his father got out, pulled the chair from the trunk, unfolded it, and wheeled it over to Harry's side of the car; the struggle to transfer himself from the bucket seat to the chair. And—most horrible on that first day—trying to control himself, trying not to scream at his father to get away, not to touch him, not to help him. And everyone either watching, or pretending not to. It was almost a relief to wheel himself, alone, up the wide wooden ramp into school.

Everyone else stuck to the steps, of course. He'd felt them there the first day, hanging out, staring. He hadn't looked at anyone, had gone straight into the building. Early, before the bell, like the nerds who had nothing better to do than sit in home-room before they absolutely had to be there.

They had arranged his schedule so that all his classes were on the ground floor and he wouldn't have to deal with stairs. They'd even moved a cou-ple of classes onto the ground floor so Harry could be in them. The principal, Loretta LoBianco, had been so pleased with herself about this that Harry had wanted to smack her.

On that first day back, he'd found his home-room, 107, and yes, there she'd been, Queen Nerd in all her glory—okay, not exactly in the room but right outside so that under no circumstances would she risk being late. She was standing with that friend of hers, Paulina, and they were listen-ing to Felicia Goren. Oh, right, that Jason Shepherd stuff. Alison had told him about her lit-tle problem. He didn't know why. How was he sup-posed to know whether Jason Shepherd really wanted to ask Alison out? Or maybe he was sup-posed to be impressed? Well, he didn't care about Jason Shepherd and Felicia Goren and their stupid in-crowd politics. He had his own problems.

The girls hadn't seen him. Felicia Goren flicked her blond hair back with one long-nailed hand. Alison and Paulina listened. When Felicia finally paused for breath, Alison shook her head. She turned toward the classroom door, and noticed him.

"Hi," she said cautiously. She held her books very still before her in her arms.

After a second, Harry nodded at her, then looked away. He turned his chair and went on into homeroom. Nobody was there yet, of course, and all the desks were attached to chairs. Great. Loretta LoBianco was really on top of things. Maybe he could snag a tray from the cafeteria, use that as a desk. He wheeled in farther, stopping near the back beside the first row of desks. It would have to do.

"So what's your schedule?" said Alison.

She had followed him in. Stubborn little bitch. He tried to feel angry, but it was too much of a relief not to be alone. Harry watched her sit down at the desk next to him. She was wearing regular Levi's and a white T-shirt with lace trim. Tiny pearl earrings and that ponytail.

Maybe Jason Shepherd really did want to ask her out.

Harry unhooked his backpack from the chair arm, reached in, and handed her his schedule. He watched her look at it. Other kids were coming in now, talking, laughing. He knew some of them from last year, but not all. A couple nodded to him, but no one came over. But then, no one had visited him at the hospital. Not even the guys he'd played sports with. Certainly not the great Jason Shepherd, who wasn't bad at defense but couldn't shoot if his life depended on it.

"You're in my English class," Alison was saying. Her ponytail had swung over to the left side of her face and was hanging down, almost touching his schedule as she studied it. "And math, first period." She looked at Harry doubtfully. "We're doing trig."

"The rest of the class is, maybe," Harry said nastily. "But you're not, are you?" She thought he was stupid. He had always known she thought he was stupid. It stuck out all over her, how stupid she thought other people were. It felt good to be mad at her.

Alison stared at him. The bell rang. The rest of the kids in homeroom rushed in; a girl Harry had never seen before came up and looked at Harry curiously while waiting, ostentatiously, for Alison to get out of her seat and go across to her own. Mr. Grandison took attendance, after which Harry was kept busy fielding his advances and concern. By the time the bell rang for first period, and Alison came back over, frowning, Harry was ready.

"What do you mean I'm not doing what the rest of the class is?" she began. "How do you know? You haven't been there!"

They started down the corridor toward math. It

was amazing, Harry thought, how Alison never noticed anything. Right now she was so busy glaring at him that she didn't even see how people were looking at them. "Don't yell," he said pleasantly. It wasn't so bad. If she was that absorbed, he could pretend to be equally so. If she didn't notice all the other kids, he'd pretend he didn't either.

Obediently, she lowered her voice. "What did you mean by it?"

They'd arrived outside the math room, but still had a couple of minutes before the bell. "I was in your math class last year. Mrs. Atterbury never asked you questions like everybody else. And you always folded up your homework before handing it up the aisle, but I saw it once, and it wasn't what we were doing. And you stayed after a lot and had a different math book in your bag all year. And Mrs. Atterbury acting like you were God's gift." Harry smirked up into Alison's stricken face. "Doesn't take a rocket scientist, Shandling. Why the hell don't they skip you, anyway?"

"But only Paulina—"

The bell rang. "We'll be late," said Harry sweetly. He watched Alison grit her teeth in frustration.

All that first day back at school she pestered him, showing up briefly even between the classes they didn't share, upset, wanting to know how much he'd figured out about her. Secretly, Harry was grateful. He never had to go alone from one class to another, didn't have to fumble with his tray at lunch—she just grabbed two, still talking, not even giving him a chance to protest—or, alone, search for a place to sit. More, her presence gave the day shape, distracted him a little from the other kids, from the classes in which, as his father had predicted, he was badly behind despite the tutoring, and from the horror and pity and curiosity and malice he saw everywhere.

And the best part of all was how oblivious she was.

The rest of the week, Harry kept an eye, too, on Jason Shepherd. Shepherd sat right behind Alison in math class—Shandling, Shepherd, everyone but Harry was in strict alphabetical order—and he was playing it cool, but there was definitely something going on. Not that anything would come of it. Alison had rejected the usual channels, and Shepherd wasn't going to risk ridicule by asking out some nerd who might say no.

Harry thought it was actually pretty funny to watch—especially since he'd taken care, at lunch that first day, to tell Alison she'd done the right thing. Shepherd, used to being pursued, was waiting with growing impatience for Alison to show interest. He'd fidget in his chair, and once even jostled the back of hers with his desk. And, to Harry's glee, he'd ask every day about her math homework—which, of course, drove Alison crazy with the suspicion she was being mocked. *Do you think he knows about the extra work I do?* she'd whisper to Harry later. *He'd tell everyone. It'd be awful.*

Clueless, his Queen Nerd. Just totally out of it.

On Saturday morning Harry woke up early. He stayed in bed anyway, waiting for his father to leave for the synagogue. They had stopped talking about whether Harry would go too. Harry supposed Alison would be there, but that wasn't enough to make him go. And anyway, Alison would be with her family. The Mad Professor. And his wife who'd been here last Sunday, drinking coffee in the kitchen, eyeballing Harry like he was some lower species of life. And that creepy kid that his own father was so nutty on. Alison's twin brother.

Harry got up as soon as he heard his father leave. It was one of those gorgeous April days that felt like May—the kind of Saturday it had always killed him to waste by going to synagogue, hanging out with his father playing Scrabble or some other half-assed game. Well, at least that was over for good.

But it wasn't as if he was free now. In the old days he would've been outside on a day like today. He might have gone down to the park and found some guys to play ball with. He wondered what some random guys at the park would say if he showed up now.

He thought about calling Zee. He'd run into him a few times at the hospital. Once or twice they'd been there at the same time for physical therapy, and had stayed later to play one-on-one at the gym. But it was different, running into Zee like that. He didn't think he could call him. Anyway, it was stupid. Zee lived south of Boston, in Milton. He couldn't get there, not by himself. Could Zee get to him? It didn't matter. Zee wasn't really his friend.

"Do you have any friends?" Dr. Jefferies had asked once.

She had not meant the guys Harry used to hang out with. They'd hung out with him because he was good at sports. They did some stuff together, but not outside of school.

"Paulina's my best friend," Alison had said, last Thursday. "Since I was little." They'd been in the cafeteria. It was the one day Paulina had the same lunch period as Alison. Paulina had come in with her tray and seen Alison sitting with Harry. Alison waved at her, and Paulina had waved back, but then she'd gone over and sat down at the table by the windows, with Felicia Goren and some other girls. Harry hadn't said anything. He didn't like Paulina de Silva any more than she liked him. And Alison was perfectly free to go sit wherever she wanted. He hadn't asked her to sit with him.

He'd almost laughed when Alison asked him if he liked Felicia. He didn't know why she thought his opinion of Felicia mattered. She'd seemed comforted, though, when he said no.

He didn't know what was in her head. Why was

she hanging around with him, anyway? Why wasn't she with her best friend, eating lunch with Felicia Goren, putting the moves on Jason Shepherd? Alison wasn't his friend, either. He couldn't mention her name to Dr. Jefferies. He couldn't call Alison. Could he?

He stared outside, felt the breeze coming through the window he'd just opened. She was just a nerd, after all. And she'd started this. She'd hung out with him all week at school. Did it matter why? And she lived close enough to come over.

The Shandlings would be home by noon, he figured. And his father would be at the synagogue all day. Keeping out of Harry's way. Well, that was fine with Harry. Better than fine.

He'd get dressed and have breakfast. Hang out. Then, later, if he felt like it, he'd call Alison.

Just before one o'clock, Alison arrived. Harry was outside waiting, tossing a basketball in the air, juggling it between his hands. He felt wonderful. "Hey, Shandling," he called out as soon as he saw her approaching on her bike. "It's a B-ball day. Knew it the minute I got outside. Let's go! There's a court in the park a couple blocks over. You can leave your bike here." He wheeled out onto the sidewalk to meet her.

Alison dismounted, walked her bike over to the side of Harry's house as he indicated, and leaned it up against the garage. She turned back to Harry, frowning. She had a pocketbook with her. Why did she want to haul a pocketbook around on such a beautiful day? And it was bulging out on one side with a shape suspiciously rectangular, like a book. A book. When they'd agreed on the phone to do something outdoors. Well, at least she was predictable. He sort of liked that. But she definitely needed a little shaking up.

"I was thinking we could take a walk," she was saying. "Maybe down to the cemetery. I passed it on the way here. It looked really pretty. The forsythia's out."

"Forsythia?" said Harry. *Cemetery*? he thought.

"It's a flowering tree. I can't believe you don't know it. Look—there's one over there in that front yard." Alison pointed. "Isn't it pretty?"

"Oh, right, yeah, that yellow stuff. Forsythia." He paused. "Okay, so great, we saw it. Now we can go play hoops. Everybody's happy."

Alison didn't look happy. Harry tried a smile on her. Nothing. "C'mon," he said. "Please? Huh?"

It worked. Alison grinned back, if reluctantly. Harry felt a sudden spurt of pleasure with himself. "Oh, all right," she said. Harry handed her the ball. She held it as if it were an unexploded bomb. They started off.

"You're sure there'll be some guys there for you to play with?" Alison asked after a while. "I guess

I don't really mind. I have a book, of course. And it's nice to read outdoors."

Oho. She thought she was going to read. Harry couldn't control himself. He laughed out loud. Hell, she probably thought a cemetery was just a big outdoor library with a lot of backrests. Queen Nerd paradise. Well, okay. She was young. Harry wouldn't tell her different. She was a case, wasn't she? He bet Dr. Jefferies could have just as much fun snooping around in Alison's brain as she did with Harry's. He snickered again.

"What are you laughing at?" Alison squinted at him suspiciously.

They'd reached the park. Two guys were playing one-on-one on half the court, but the other end was still free. Good. Harry stopped his chair on that end, claiming it.

"I'm laughing at you," he said to Alison. She looked surprised for a moment, then indignant. "Give me your bag."

"What?"

"Give it to me. And don't look so worried." He took the pocketbook from her. "I'll give it back later." He opened the backpack hanging on the side of his chair and shoved the bag down in there, deep. "When you've earned it."

"What are you talking about? My book's in there!"

"We are here," said Harry, slowly, deliberately,

"to play some ball. Get some exercise. Outdoor activity, Shandling. You don't need your book."

"Wait. You expect *me* to play with you?"

"Amazing. Must be that famous Shandling brain." Harry tapped the side of his head with his index finger and nodded knowingly.

"Don't you make fun of me!" Alison had flushed. She looked pretty like that. She was clenching her fists at her sides. They were the wrong kind of fists, Harry noted idly. She had her thumbs tucked inside; if she ever really tried to hit someone like that, she'd break them. "You know I don't do sports! Play with those guys over there. I'm no good!"

"Well," said Harry, "I'm only a cripple. So you're starting small."

She stared at him, horror clear on her face. It was that word. "Cripple." It hung in the air between them. She'd never used it. Neither, Harry realized, had he. Not out loud. Not with her, not with anyone. It had popped out like a jack-in-the-box.

"You know you'll still beat me," Alison said after a pause.

"Even though I'm a cripple?" He said it again, on purpose this time, experimenting. He hadn't choked, had he? She still looked scared. "Huh?"

"Yes."

He looked at her. He waited. The silence lengthened.

"Even though you're a cripple," she said finally. "Is that what you wanted me to say? Well, are you happy?"

He *was* happy. Harry was suddenly, gloriously, irrationally happy. "Yeah," he said. "I'll beat you. But that doesn't matter. It's not about winning." He spun around, heading closer to the basket. "Come on. I'll show you some moves. You're probably not as bad as you think you are. Attitude is real important in sports, and, to be frank, Queen Nerd, yours sucks. We can work on that."

After a minute, dazed, Alison followed Harry.

ALISON • April

After dinner that night, Alison helped Adam clear the dishes from the table and load them into the dishwasher. Adam measured and put in the soap, closed the washer's Plexiglas see-through door, and started the washing cycle. Then he sat down on the floor in front of the washer and watched it. Alison hesitated and then, abruptly, sat down next to him. She saw Adam glance at her and away. He didn't smile, just accepted her presence and ignored her, focusing on the dishwasher. It was as companionable as Adam ever got.

The jets at the top of the dishwasher were revolving, shooting out water in a slightly jerky motion onto the dishes below. It was a reliable little machine. It would clean up the mess. Alison wondered if it could do anything with her life.

Alison's life was a mess. Today, Saturday, she had again not seen Paulina. She'd called, but Paulina hadn't been in. "I'm sorry, Alison," Mrs. de Silva had said. "Paulina went to the mall. I thought...I thought you were going too? With that girl Felicia?"

"No," Alison replied. She'd said good-bye and hung up quickly, before Mrs. de Silva's voice could get any more concerned. Felicia. She'd stood there a few moments, stunned, and her hand had still been on the receiver when the telephone rang. It was Harry. He'd sounded like she felt. Unsure. Defensive. He'd asked what she was doing, she'd said nothing, and in the end she'd biked over. Just like that.

It had seemed both utterly normal and utterly bizarre, going to visit Harry. She hadn't told her parents. It was risky to let them think she was at Paulina's, because her mother was so friendly with Mrs. de Silva.

But Alison couldn't explain to her mother. Not about Harry. And not even about Paulina. She didn't know why Paulina was acting this way. Was she mad about Jason Shepherd? Or about Harry? Alison knew it had probably looked weird to Paulina—all the time she'd spent with Harry at school in the past week. Alison hadn't explained to Paulina about Harry. She didn't quite know how. Things had happened so fast—and so differently from what she'd expected. Even if she could explain, Paulina couldn't possibly understand.

The fact was, Alison had set out deliberately to befriend Harry. She had never done that with anyone else. She'd seen other kids who did, kids who hung around persistently on the fringes of crowds they wanted to belong to—like Paulina these days.

But Harry wasn't a crowd; he was all alone. Once she'd thought he was friendly with those other kids, or at least with some of them. But he wasn't, and he was hurt.

Alison looked at her brother. The dishwasher was now full of soapy water, with more water shooting down hard from the top onto the dishes; Adam was completely absorbed in watching. When she was little, Alison had wondered if Adam had done anything to deserve being autistic. If God had done it to him. She had asked her mother, who had been aghast. It's not his fault, Mrs. Shandling had said. God doesn't punish people that way.

What does He do then? Alison wondered now. Just sit there and let awful stuff happen to people for no reason?

Buddhists believed that you paid in your current life for sins in your last life. Rabbi Roth believed that God had punished Harry for his father's mistake about Adam. And her own father didn't believe in God at all, just in science.

She wondered what Harry would think about all

this. She wondered what he would think if he understood that Alison felt responsible for him and for what had happened. If he realized that Alison had begun to hang around with him because she felt that, like it or not, she had to do something.

Because no one else—including Harry's father, and including God—would.

They had gone for a walk that afternoon, after Alison had made enough of an idiot of herself, dribbling and throwing the ball at the basket, to make Harry happy. It was true she had gotten a basket or two after Harry insisted she try it with her glasses on. But Alison had not been comfortable. What if the ball fell on her face and broke her glasses? It wasn't safe.

"Contact lenses," said Harry after they left the park and started back. "They're perfect for sports. You have them, don't you?"

"Yes," said Alison doubtfully. She didn't like wearing contacts. She liked her glasses. The wire frames were green and funky with tiny flecks of silver on them.

"Wear the contacts," said Harry, as if that settled it.

Alison said nothing. They went on in silence for a while. Then, when they came up to the cemetery and Alison paused, looking in at the forsythia,

Harry asked, "Do you really want to snoop around in there?"

Alison nodded. "It's peaceful."

Harry snorted. But he swiveled his chair, and they went in.

It was a Christian cemetery, well kept and beautifully landscaped, with crosses embedded on lots of gravestones and no little stones left on top for remembrance. But there were flowers, and Alison noticed a spot that would be good for reading. "Under that tree. It's shady, but there's plenty of grass, and you could lean up against the tree. Or against that big vault thing."

"Vault?" Harry was looking at it like he'd never seen one before.

"Yeah, the little building." She paused awkwardly, suddenly remembering about Harry's mother. "It's...for a whole family. I think."

"What?" Harry seemed fascinated. "You mean the caskets go in there instead of in the ground?"

"I think so."

Harry stared at the vault. "That's disgusting."

Alison shrugged. Harry's face looked very odd. Alison felt increasingly strange. She began to wish she had never mentioned the cemetery.

"I can't believe it," Harry said after a long minute. He was still staring at the vault. "Why would anyone want to do that? Do you know what that means? Huh?" He swung his chair around to face Alison. "Every time somebody died, you'd have to open it up, and you'd have to go in there, and...What do you do then, huh, Shandling? D'you say, 'Hey, hello there, Mom, company! Here's Dad!'" He paused, trembling.

"I think only really rich people do it," said Alison, inanely. She was sorry the minute she'd said it.

"Stupid rich people," said Harry.

Alison said nothing. There was a huge knot in her stomach. She wanted to get out of the cemetery.

"I'm going to get burned," said Harry abruptly. He had turned away from Alison again. "I'm going to have them cremate me, and then I'll have someone scatter the ashes. No coffin, no gravestone. Nothing."

Alison wondered if Harry thought about death a lot. Did he think about death as often as she thought about Adam and God and responsibility? "I know what you mean," she said.

Harry started; he looked at Alison as if he had forgotten she was there and didn't like being reminded. "No, you don't," he said. His voice went hostile on her. "You—Queen Nerd. You may know a lot of math, but you don't know fucking anything about what's really important. Hanging out in cemeteries. You're so stupid, it's pathetic."

Harry turned his chair and started back down

the path toward the cemetery gate. Alison stood stunned, staring after him. She inhaled sharply.

Just who the hell did Harry Roth think he was, anyway? Alison heard the "hell" in her head with satisfaction; she suddenly understood why Harry swore so much. It let people know you were mad. She yelled it aloud: "Who the hell do you think you are, Harry Roth?!" And she ran down the path after him, aware somewhere in her head that she was running the way Harry had just taught her at the park. She raced past Harry and then turned, stopped, put out her hands to catch his chair by the arms and halt his progress.

"Let go, you little bitch," said Harry. He continued to push on his wheels. Alison pushed back in the other direction as hard as she could. She was leaning forward, panting, her face practically touching Harry's. He glared at her as he continued to try to force the chair forward. Alison pushed back just as hard, and they came to a standstill.

"Give it up!" Harry yelled.

Alison kept shoving. It felt good. She yelled back. "You think you're the only cripple in the world, Harry Roth? You think you're the only person with problems? Well, grow up!" She yelled it right in his face. "Just *fucking* grow up!"

Abruptly, Harry stopped trying to wheel the chair forward. Caught off guard, Alison's own momentum threw her forward on top of him. She stared into Harry's eyes for a paralyzed second. Overbalanced, the chair teetered. Then it tipped, toppling them both over onto the pebbled walk.

Alison didn't even have time to scream. She landed quite safely, half on top of Harry, half on top of the chair. Frightened, she stared at him. She saw him looking back at her, his eyes as angry, as startled, as shocked, as hers. She felt his body under hers. And she saw his eyes change, into...into something. Awareness? For a moment she couldn't move, couldn't speak.

Then she rolled away, fast. She scrambled to her knees on the path, pushing the chair away.

"Say something. Are you okay?"

After an endless moment Harry spoke. "Shit," he said.

Alison thought that meant he was okay. He looked pissed off, too pissed off to be hurt. "I'm sorry," she said. Her mind started to clear. They hadn't landed very hard, really. "Are you hurt? Can you move?"

"I don't feel like moving," Harry said. "God, you're stupid."

"I am not!" Alison snapped back, relieved. It felt good to be angry again, to leave that odd little moment of awareness behind. "And anyway, you asked for it!" She stopped in horror. But no, it was okay, Harry was shifting his torso and arms. Then he pushed himself up to a sitting position, keeping his legs straight out in front of him, putting his hands behind and leaning on them. Alison watched. His arms were shaking slightly.

"What the fuck are you staring at?"

"There's a tree two inches behind you," Alison said. "You could lean against that." For a second she thought Harry would be too stubborn to listen, but then he did lean back a little, slowly, until he had his back against the tree trunk. He stared at Alison, defiant, the whole time.

"You're going to have to get me back in the chair."

"Of course—" Alison started to say, and then she narrowed her eyes. "No. First you take it back."

"Take what back? That you're stupid?" Harry looked scornful.

"No. The other thing you said—that I don't know what's really important." Alison adjusted her position on the ground, sitting, pulling her legs up in front of her, and encircling them with her arms. She stared defiantly at Harry. He was the stupid one. He never thought about anyone but himself. "You take it back," she said. "Go ahead. Do it."

"Why should I?" Harry was incredulous.

"Because you know better," Alison said. "All week I thought about you. Do you think that was easy? Do you think after everything you said last year—about my being a nerd, and about my brother—that it was easy? Huh? Do you think it was easy being nice to you?"

"I never asked you for anything," Harry said. He had gone pale.

"No," Alison said. "You didn't—"

"And it's not any of your business," Harry said. He wasn't looking at her now. He was looking away, at the chair turned on its side, out of his reach. And suddenly Alison realized she had made a terrible mistake. She had told Harry he was obligated to her. And unless she said something now to make it okay, Harry would be gone, beyond her reach, left alone at school—left alone, period.

Somehow it was important to her that that not happen.

She put her head down, cheek pressing against her knees, no longer looking at Harry. "You used to call my brother a retard," she said finally. She wasn't sure why she was talking about Adam. "But he isn't. He's autistic. Nobody is really sure what that means, but Adam's smart about a lot of stuff. He's better at some number stuff than I am, even." She paused. "My mother says he doesn't have a lot of social skills. Sort of like me, maybe. Nerds aren't too social.

"He's my twin brother, you know," she said finally.

"So?" Harry said. His voice was quiet, unemphatic.

"So don't say I don't think about important things."

"Okay," said Harry, after a long while. "I won't."

Alison raised her head from her knees. Harry was facing her again. He was still pale. She scrubbed at her eyes. He watched. And then, quietly, he said, "I still don't understand what you're doing here with me."

"I know," said Alison. She was suddenly exhausted. "It's not my business."

They looked at each other in silence for another moment. Then Harry spoke. "Well, it isn't," he said.

Alison took a deep breath. "I've made it my business," she said, simply.

They were quiet.

"I don't like cemeteries," Harry said finally. "Do you think you could help me into my chair?"

Alison looked dubiously at the overturned chair.

"Look, I know what to do," said Harry. "I just need a little help."

"I'll try," said Alison. She looked at Harry.

He looked back.

Neither smiled.

HARRY · April

"Do you know anything about autism?" Harry asked Dr. Jefferies.

They were in the middle of their Tuesday afternoon session, with Dr. Jefferies asking the usual sorts of questions about Harry's father and school, while Harry parried with as few words as possible. Silences were hallmarks of their sessions; this particular one had gone on for nearly four minutes before Harry, to his own surprise, interrupted it.

He could see Dr. Jefferies was surprised too. She leaned forward, and the words "Why do you—" came out before she stopped herself. She sat back. "I know a little about it," she said.

Harry waited, watching her watch him. "Could you please tell me what little you know?" he said, politely.

For some reason Dr. Jefferies smiled. She looked off into space for a moment and then looked back at Harry. She said slowly, "Autism is still an enigma. We don't know exactly what it is or what causes it. It's really just a name given to people, often children, who share some odd behaviors—"

"Like what?"

"Well, one common autistic behavior is not talking, or just echoing back what other people say. An autistic child seems to have difficulty learning that words have meaning. The child might even appear deaf."

Harry shook his head. Alison's brother wasn't like that.

Dr. Jefferies was watching him carefully. "That's only one kind of autistic behavior. Some autistics grow out of that stage, though I think they might always have trouble with pronunciation or with voice tone." She paused. "Does that sound more familiar?"

"Maybe," said Harry. "Go on."

"Another key thing is that autistics seem to be in their own world. They don't interact normally with other people, dislike being touched, behave oddly in social situations. And some autistic people may also be retarded." Dr. Jefferies paused. She gave Harry a straight look. "Harry, this is a big subject. Help me out. I can concentrate on what you want to know if you'll tell me what that is."

He didn't really have a choice. "I know this boy," he said carefully, after a minute. "His sister says he's autistic."

"Tell me about him."

"He does act strange. I always thought he was retarded, but he's not stupid, you know? He's going to have a bar mitzvah, and my father says..."

"What does your father say?"

"That he's really bright. Adam—that's his name—picked up Hebrew like it was nothing, and he's already mostly memorized his Haftorah portion. He came over to our house for a lesson last Sunday, and I heard him singing it."

Dr. Jefferies nodded. "Sometimes autistics have special skills. A fantastic memory or the ability to play music by ear. Or great mathematical talent. It's almost as though it's to make up for the other losses. It sounds like this boy, Adam, may have some of these abilities."

Harry nodded, thinking. They sat in silence for a few moments.

"Harry?" said Dr. Jefferies gently. "Why are you so interested in this boy?"

Harry sat up, startled. "I'm not!" he snapped. "His sister—" He broke off. Shit, he thought.

"His sister?" said Dr. Jefferies. "You mentioned her before. What's her name?"

"Forget it," said Harry. "It's not important."

"Does she go to your school?" Dr. Jefferies persisted.

"Yeah."

"Is she a friend of yours?"

No, thought Harry. I don't know. Maybe. "She cares about her brother," he said. It just came out, the way his question about autism had. He stared at Dr. Jefferies defiantly.

"She sounds very nice," Dr. Jefferies said quietly. "This girl. Adam's sister."

Harry stared at Dr. Jefferies. Then he looked away.

There was another silence. Harry could feel Dr. Jefferies looking at him, could feel her trying to work her way into his head. Finally she spoke. "Harry? You said your father is getting Adam ready for a bar mitzvah?"

Harry looked up. "Yes."

"I'm a little puzzled. Is that part of his job, training kids for bar mitzvahs?"

Harry shook his head. "Not usually. There are tutors who do it for most kids."

"Then why—"

"I don't know," Harry interrupted. He didn't say that he'd been wondering himself. "Maybe nobody else would do it. I don't know. Okay?"

"You sound a little tense."

"Why don't you just—" Harry swallowed what he'd been about to say. "I don't know why he's tutoring Adam himself," he repeated, slowly, word by word.

Dr. Jefferies considered that. Then she asked, "Do you have any theories?"

"No," Harry said. Who did she think he was, Sigmund Freud? Theories. Yeah, he had a theory. His father liked Adam because the kid did just what he was told. Parroted Hebrew right back. No attitude. And when the lesson was over, he went home and left the rabbi alone.

After the session, Harry called The Ride. For once, they had a van near the hospital, and it arrived fairly quickly. But there were two other passengers to be dropped off first, so it would be a long drive. Harry didn't care. He settled his chair far back in the van, so the others wouldn't talk to him, and stared out the window as the van left the hospital and headed over the Charles River. He wanted to think.

Dr. Jefferies's definition of autism sounded like Adam, all right, but knowing more about autism hadn't helped Harry. He still didn't understand what Alison had meant the other day in the cemetery. Why was she hanging around him after the way he'd treated her? She'd talked about her brother, but what did Adam and his autism have to do with Harry?

Dr. Jefferies had a good point: What was Adam

doing at Harry's house, learning Hebrew from his father and getting trained for a bar mitzvah? His father had never before tutored one on one—not even Harry. What were his reasons?

Of course, his father had mooned over Adam right from the first time he'd seen him at the synagogue. Harry closed his eyes briefly. Then, determinedly, he turned his thoughts back to Alison.

At the cemetery, after she'd talked about her brother, she'd said she'd made Harry her business. But she hadn't said why, and Harry hadn't asked.

Is she a friend of yours? Dr. Jefferies had asked.

Once Harry would have said that someone like Alison Shandling could never be his friend. But he was starting to understand her. Even the really weird stuff about her, like being a math brain.

She had spoken about that only yesterday, during lunch in the cafeteria. He'd been looking at her math book. Indecipherable stuff with strange-looking equations.

"It's interesting to me," Alison had said, watching.

Harry had rolled his eyes. "I just don't get it."

She'd wrinkled her brow, and then, to Harry's astonishment, tried to explain. "I guess...this'll sound weird, but math is almost a *place* to me ... a place—a universe, really—where everything makes sense. Or would if we knew more. You can't see this universe with your eyes, but the more you

• 152 •

learn, the more clearly you can see it without your eyes. It's real. And it's so beautiful." She'd paused, and then, unexpectedly, smiled. He'd been staring at her. "I know you think I'm nuts," she'd said. "But that's okay."

But he had not been thinking that. He had been feeling—almost jealous. "I don't think you're nuts," he had said, slowly. "Just—you're really on your own planet."

Alison had looked surprised. "Isn't everyone?" she had said. "When you think about it?"

It was a new idea for Harry. He had had a sudden vision of his father, alone on a planet, spinning in space with the ghost of his wife, trapped there.

In that moment, staring at Alison, Harry had had the odd sense that a puzzle piece had slipped, finally, into place.

Not that it helped.

ALISON • May

With half an ear, Alison listened while Adam
sang. His voice traveled clearly through the open
door of his bedroom, down the hall, and into the
study where her mother was finishing a term
paper and Alison was checking through the bar
mitzvah invitation list one last time. Adam prac-
ticed chanting his Haftorah portion every day at
four o'clock for exactly half an hour, and Alison
could almost have sung along with him by now.
With his bar mitzvah still two weeks away, Adam
was word, if not note, perfect.

The invitations had gone out nearly two weeks
ago, and responses were pouring in. Her father had
put Alison in charge of tabulating them so that they
could give a final count to the caterer. He had taken
over the whole process—guest list, invitation selec-

tion and ordering, mailing, responses, hotel arrangements for out-of-towners, everything.

Alison hadn't realized that Adam's bar mitzvah was going to be such a big deal. At first, her mother had spoken of a small affair, maybe fifty close relatives and friends, with a buffet luncheon at the house after the service. "My mother and Rosalie will help," Mrs. Shandling had said. "Crudités and dip, pasta salad, cold chicken, French bread. Maybe gazpacho..."

But this was before Alison's father had taken a turn with the invitation list. He had added nearly a hundred names. His entire department at Harvard. Relatives Alison barely knew existed, like Great-Aunt Muriel and several cousins called Eckenwiler. Their autism family support group, and the neighbors from whom the Shandlings occasionally borrowed folding chairs. The principal and vice principal of Adam's school.

"Wow," Alison had said, reading the new list over her mother's shoulder. Her mother had simply shaken her head as her husband began talking about caterers and a sit-down lunch at the synagogue.

"Caterers cost forty or fifty dollars a plate, Jake," her mother had said.

"So what?" Alison's father had replied. "We're rich."

Alison had been a little shocked. It was true, she

supposed, but it wasn't something her parents usually mentioned. And, except for buying their house and talking more about mutual funds and stuff, her parents didn't act any differently now than before the Sphere. Her mother still shopped the sales.

She'd watched her mother stare at her father, and then smile. "Okay, honey," Mrs. Shandling had said. "Go ahead. Invite the president. The Kennedys. Call the *Boston Globe*."

"I just might," Professor Shandling had said seriously. "I never dreamed Adam would have a bar mitzvah."

Watching her father's face, for a tiny moment Alison had felt like crying.

Just the other night at dinner, Alison had noticed that Adam's wrists were sticking too far out of his long-sleeved rugby shirt. Suddenly he had started growing, and you could already see that he was going to be lanky like their father. It was difficult to think about Adam growing up. That was what a bar mitzvah was about, really. And if it was a scary thought for Alison, it must be even scarier for her parents. Because Adam was never going to be normal, no matter how many bar mitzvahs he had. Alison was in charge of doing all the normal things for both of them.

In a few years, Adam was going to be an autistic man, not an autistic child. Alison wondered what that would mean. Would he be interested in girls? One day, would he be able to get some kind of job, have an apartment, the way her parents hoped?

It was no wonder that her father wanted the bar mitzvah to be such a big deal. You had to celebrate what you could.

Even Harry had been invited. "We have to," Mrs. Shandling had said apologetically to Alison. "Because of his father. Honey, I'm sorry. But he's not bothering you these days, is he?"

"No," Alison had said, feeling guilty.

"Good." Mrs. Shandling had grimaced and turned away. "Nasty young man. Anyway, Paulina will be there for you."

Remembering, Alison felt another twinge of guilt. It wasn't only about Harry. She and Paulina now hadn't spoken in nearly three weeks. She checked the last name off on the invitation list. She glanced at her mother, still deeply immersed in her work. Down the hall, Adam was winding down, moving from the Haftorah section to the blessings that followed.

What was she supposed to say to her mother, anyway? *Paulina's got a new best friend, Mom. She likes Felicia better than me because Felicia's popular. But I've been hanging out with Harry, and he's not so bad. I think I'm starting to understand why he acts the way he does. He's sort of like me. He keeps a lot of stuff to himself....*

No. She wouldn't say anything. They were occupied with Adam, anyway. They wouldn't notice Alison.

That had always been how it was, and it was best.

Wasn't it?

After school on the day before Adam's bar mitzvah, Alison rode home with Harry in the van. Adam was due at the Roths' for one last rehearsal with the rabbi. "I'll just meet Adam there after school," Alison had told her mother. "You can pick us both up there after Adam's lesson." Her mother had agreed. It didn't seem to have occurred to her that Adam now knew Rabbi Roth well; he no longer needed Alison there too.

"Hello," Rabbi Roth called, as they came in the door. Harry didn't reply. He gestured Alison toward the kitchen. Alison hesitated, calling out "Hello, Rabbi Roth" before following Harry.

"Chocolate pudding?" asked Harry, investigating the contents of the refrigerator. "There are a couple left."

"Sure," said Alison. She took two spoons out of the dish drainer and handed one to Harry before sitting down. The pudding was instant, and it hadn't been mixed too well; there was still powder around the edges. But it was edible.

She felt a little awkward here at the house with

Harry. Coming home with him felt different from the times when she'd come over with Adam. Different, too, from seeing Harry at school, even though they'd been spending a lot of time together there. She looked at Harry. He had already finished his pudding and had pushed the empty dish away. He was drumming his fingers on the table, not looking at Alison. She wondered if he felt strange too, with her there.

Rabbi Roth came into the kitchen just as Alison was swallowing the last of her pudding. "Nice to see you, Alison," he said to her. "I guess your brother is due here in a few minutes." Alison nodded. She noticed Rabbi Roth was frowning at the two empty dishes on the table.

"Is there any pudding left?" he asked Harry.

"Nope," said Harry.

Rabbi Roth went and looked in the refrigerator himself, as if he didn't believe Harry. "Adam likes chocolate pudding," he said. He lifted out the milk carton and shook it accusingly. "There isn't enough milk to make more."

"Well," Harry said, "that's too bad. Will he starve, do you think?" He and his father glared at each other.

Alison squirmed.

There was a short silence. Then Rabbi Roth closed the refrigerator door and took a deep breath. After a moment, he moved his lips in the facsimile of a smile. "Well," he said. "How was school today, Harry? Alison? You helping him catch up?"

Alison looked at Harry. He looked back at her, his face expressionless. It was true that she was helping Harry a little. But she knew better than to say anything. She shrugged. "School's fine," she said. "You know."

"No," said Rabbi Roth pleasantly. He leaned forward and spoke directly to Alison, ignoring Harry. "I really don't. My son doesn't talk to me about school. He doesn't like it. He doesn't make A's like you."

Alison wanted to die.

The doorbell rang. "That must be my brother," said Alison.

"Excuse me," said Rabbi Roth.

Alison listened as Rabbi Roth opened the front door and welcomed Adam. She didn't look at Harry. "Hi, Adam," she called instead, after a moment.

Adam appeared in the kitchen doorway with Rabbi Roth. "Hello, Alison Shandling," said Adam. "Hello, Harold Roth. Hello, hello, hello. I want orange juice. One half."

Alison felt like laughing. Thank God, she thought, he doesn't want pudding. She sneaked a glance at Harry.

"Hello, Adam Shandling," Harry was saying. "There's orange juice. One half."

"I'll pour," said Rabbi Roth, beginning to bustle around the kitchen. Finally he and Adam took the orange juice and headed down the hall to the den. A minute later Alison heard the beginning strains of Adam's bar mitzvah portion.

"Let's go to my room," said Harry.

From behind the closed door of Harry's bedroom, the sounds of Adam's and Rabbi Roth's voices were still audible, but easy to ignore. Alison felt a renewed surge of awkwardness. That scene with Harry's father. Should she say something?

Harry had rolled his chair over near his bed and was pulling books out of his backpack, throwing them onto the bed. "Let's look at the math," he said. He swiveled a little and glanced at Alison, standing near the door. "Okay with you?"

He didn't want to talk about it. Alison went and sat on the bed, opening the math book at an angle in front of her so that both she and Harry could see it. "Okay," she said. "The simultaneous equations?"

"Yeah."

"They're a rote thing," said Alison. "You do the same things in the same order, and they come out every time. Watch." She did the first homework problem. "See? Try the next one. All you have to do is follow the rules." In the background, she heard Rabbi Roth say something. Then Adam started reciting in Hebrew.

"I hate rules," said Harry. He made no move to

take the pencil Alison was holding out to him. After a minute, she put it down.

"Sports have rules," she said reasonably.

Harry gave her a look. He reached out with one hand and slammed the math book shut.

Adam began singing his Haftorah portion again.

"I can't stand it," said Harry abruptly. "No offense, Shandling, but I've heard that goddamned Haftorah so many times in the last three weeks, I've got it memorized. I'm starting to dream it."

"Me too," said Alison.

Suddenly Harry looked directly at her. "My father is fixated on your brother."

Alison shrugged helplessly. "Yeah," she said. "Pretty strange, huh?" She watched Harry carefully.

"Do you think so?" Harry said. He moved his chair a little closer to the bed. Closer to Alison.

Alison didn't back off. She wondered again if he knew his father thought God had caused Harry's accident because of Adam. "Yes," she said honestly. "I do think it's a little strange."

"I do too," said Harry. "But I don't understand why *you* think it's strange."

"Why not?" said Alison. Somehow, Harry seemed even closer now.

"Because you've been acting a lot like my father." He paused. "Do you know what I mean?"

"No," said Alison. It came out a squeak.

"He's fixated on your brother," said Harry. "And you're fixated on me." Alison couldn't move. She couldn't speak. She knew he was right.

"Isn't that true?" said Harry. His face was very close, very still.

Slowly, Alison shook her head. "It's not the same," she whispered. "You don't understand."

Harry's voice was as low as Alison's. But it held a mean edge. "Explain it to me. Use one-syllable words so you can be sure I get it."

Alison opened her mouth, but nothing came out.

"Well?" he said. "Were you being nice to the cripple because you felt sorry for him? Or what?"

"Shut up," hissed Alison. "I was starting to like you, but I—"

"Right," interrupted Harry. He imitated her voice. "I started to like you." He sneered. "Yeah, I believe that one."

Alison caught her breath in anger. "You'd better believe it," she spat back, "because it's true. You were so horrible, someone had to pay attention! And once I started paying attention..."

Harry froze. They stared at each other. And then, slowly, Harry asked: "Why? Tell me why you decided to pay attention?"

Alison swallowed. She turned her face away before she answered. "I think because—in a different way—for different reasons—no one in my family pays any attention to me either."

There was silence. Tentatively, Alison turned back to face Harry, and met his eyes. And, equally slowly, he reached out and took her head in his hands. And then leaned forward and kissed her, gently, on the forehead.

And then on the mouth.

And then backed off.

Astonished, Alison put her hand to her lips. She stared at Harry.

And he blushed. Alison watched in disbelief as the blush spread upward on his neck and washed over his entire face. He bit his lip. He turned away. "I'm out of practice," he muttered. She could barely hear him.

She said, just as quietly, "It might be easier if I helped."

In the silence Alison could hear Rabbi Roth talking. Something about responsive readings.

"You interested?" said Harry. He had turned back toward her.

"Maybe."

He waited, watching her. Alison realized she would have to make the next move. She wiped her palms surreptitiously on her jeans. Then she leaned over and kissed Harry, gently.

"You're not really in practice either, are you?" said Harry, after a minute.

"No." Alison was feeling surprised. Harry's lips were very soft. Sweet.

"It might be even easier," Harry said, "if you would sit on my lap." His voice went defensive. "It's a little hard for me to lean over."

"Oh," said Alison. "Okay." She moved. His arms came around her. They felt good. They kissed again. Practice, Alison thought, was a good idea. She heard a short rapping noise but paid no attention.

"Alison? I wonder if you could..." It was Rabbi Roth's voice. Startled, both Alison and Harry looked up, toward the door.

It was Rabbi Roth himself.

In the doorway, holding the doorknob. Staring at them.

HARRY AND ALISON • May

$\mathcal{A}$dam was doing considerably better than Harry himself had done, two years before, Harry thought, watching his father watch Adam, at the podium, as he finished his nearly perfect Haftorah portion before a congregation of hundreds of Shandling relatives, friends, and acquaintances.

He hoped that made his father, revolving on his own little planet, happy. Meanwhile, Harry himself was going to pay some attention to the planet sitting in front of him in the first row, next to her parents. Alison.

His father hadn't said anything about walking in on them yesterday. Harry had waited all day and evening and into today, right up until it was time to go to Adam's bar mitzvah, and his father hadn't said a word.

He supposed that was good. Alison had been so terrified. She had slid right off his lap and fallen on the floor, and he had wanted to laugh, but—although he would never have told Alison—he'd been startled himself. And nervous. And frustrated.

He had wanted to kiss her again.

He wanted to kiss her now.

She was wearing a white dress that was covered with lots of tiny green dots. It had a wide green bow at the waist in the back, and it looked very soft.

So far during the service, he had pulled the bow untied twice. The second time, her mother had twisted suddenly in her seat to look at him, and he had smiled directly at her.

Mrs. Shandling didn't like him at all. He could tell.

"May the Lord bless you and keep you," his father was intoning over Adam. "May the Lord let his countenance shine upon you...."

Harry watched Adam; he was actually pretty entertaining. At this point, receiving the rabbinical blessing, a bar mitzvah candidate was supposed to have his head down and his face solemn. Not Adam. He had half turned away from the rabbi and was staring back at the ark containing the Torah scrolls. He looked as if, any second, he would bolt right over there and investigate whatever it was he had noticed.

Harry wasn't the only one to notice Adam's distraction. Directly in front of Harry, the backs of all the Shandlings stiffened together. But then Adam's posture eased, he lowered his head, and the Shandlings, to a body, relaxed. And so did Harry.

He watched Adam take his seat again while the service resumed. There were only the final prayers left—fifteen minutes, maybe. Then it would be over and everyone could loosen up at last. And Harry would finally be able to talk to Alison.

Twenty minutes later, Harry tugged at his tie, wheeled halfway around on the polished wood floor to face into the synagogue's social hall, and looked around. Nearly everyone was a stranger to him, which was odd here at the synagogue. It felt good. Great, really. He could sit and look around at them all, drinking and talking to each other, and relax. There was plenty for them to look at and talk about besides him. And there weren't many kids here, either, just a few that he didn't know and, of course, Paulina.

Alison was over with her brother and parents, talking to people. That was the way these things went. He remembered. At his bar mitzvah, he'd made short work of anyone trying to talk to him. Alison wouldn't do that, of course. He grinned. More fool she.

Alison had moved a little apart from the group around her family. He caught her eye and signaled, then watched as she edged her way between groups of people toward him.

"Hi," he said, as she arrived.

"What did your father say?" she whispered. She shot a glance behind her, but most people were still milling around, or picking up the little cards with the seating assignments for lunch. Harry had already picked up his. He was at the head table. You got some privileges, being the rabbi's son.

"Nothing," Harry said.

She couldn't believe it, he could tell. There was no way that mother of hers would have said nothing. "You're lying," she said.

"He doesn't care what I do. Anyway, it's not his business." Harry added, "I had my bar mitzvah already. I'm an adult. Maybe he's treating me like one."

"But..." Alison's voice trailed off. She was looking away. "My mother's waving at me," she said. "I have to go be in the receiving line."

"See you," said Harry. He watched her hurry off.

He wondered when they could be alone again.

"Of course I remember you," Alison said for the twentieth time to the twentieth stranger. "Thank you. Yes, we're all very proud of my brother. Yes, I'm in ninth grade. Thank you. You look very nice, too." She tried not to strain to see how long the line was now. Who were all these people?

And then suddenly it was Paulina's parents, with Paulina trailing behind. Mrs. de Silva enveloped Alison in a smiling, perfumed hug. "Hello, dear," she said. "You look so lovely. Wasn't Adam terrific?"

"Hi," said Alison. "Yes. He was. We're so proud. Hello, Mr. de Silva." She submitted to being kissed. "Hi, Paulina," it hurt, sharply, to look at Paulina. They still hadn't talked.

"Hi, Alison. Congratulations."

Alison could feel Paulina's parents watching them. She wondered if Paulina had told them that she and Alison weren't hanging out together anymore, or if, like Alison, she was just letting them figure it out.

The line was stuck; up ahead, her mother and father were listening to someone with a lot to say. Adam was lucky. He had simply walked off. Alison smiled again at the de Silvas. She tried to think of something to say to them, to Paulina.

It was sad, because really she had so much to say to Paulina. About Harry, about yesterday. About what a surprise it had been, all at once. About how scared she was, and, at the same time, how...how excited—and happy. About how different Harry was, underneath, from how she had thought. About her parents, and the look on her mother's face when she had seen Harry untying the bow on Alison's dress just before Adam's Haftorah portion. About that strange man, Harry's father. About what might happen next.

She had always told Paulina nearly everything. But now it was as if they had never been close.

The de Silvas moved on.

And finally everyone had gone through the reception line, and it was time for lunch to be served.

Harry had calmly exchanged his father's and Alison's place cards at the head table so that Alison was sitting next to him, and his father was between Adam and one Dennis Shandling. He hadn't had to move his own place card; it was already in the position he would have chosen, all the way at one end of the long table, where he'd have the best maneuverability for his chair. He moved into it while everyone was still standing around talking, poured himself a glass of white wine, and ate hors d'oeuvres. The caterers were very considerate. All he had to do was wave periodically and one of them would scurry over with a tray of stuffed mushrooms or spinach canapés.

Eventually people started sitting down. Harry watched as his father came over, nodded tentatively at him, and took the seat Harry had assigned him. Not that he'd really thought there'd be any trouble there; the person to watch was Alison's mother, who was just sitting down at the table herself, her attention elsewhere.

He heard a rustling to his right. Alison. He picked up her place card and handed it to her, gesturing to the seat next to him.

"I don't think I'm supposed—" she started.

"Why not? Are you ashamed to sit next to me?"

She glanced down the table toward her mother, then sat down. "You know something?" she whispered. "You're not the most mature person I've ever met. In fact—"

"Listen," he said quietly. "I really want to kiss you again. I haven't been able to think of anything else." He felt himself reddening. He hadn't meant to say that. He hadn't meant to say anything of the kind.

Alison's voice was very low, but he could hear it. "Me, too," she said.

Lots of people came back to the house later that afternoon, and it took Alison over an hour to work her way through them and into the privacy of her own bedroom. She took some care to avoid her mother, who she had seen signaling her with puzzled eyes over the seating arrangements at lunch. But it wasn't really necessary; her mother was busy.

It was more difficult to get away from Uncle Dennis. Dennis wanted to talk about Adam.

"I mean," said Dennis, "two years ago he barely spoke at all."

"He still sometimes doesn't talk much," said

Alison. "But yeah, I guess he's changed. It's hard to tell."

"Um-hmm," Dennis said. "When you live with someone, you're always the last to notice. You have to make a conscious effort not to take him for granted." His eyes rested on his boyfriend, Gerald, who was over on the sofa talking patiently with Adam about toothpaste.

Alison squirmed. She'd known Uncle Dennis forever, of course, but somehow it was different today. She wondered what Harry would think of Dennis and Gerald. Would he think it was weird? Had he noticed them at the bar mitzvah?

If she could get to her bedroom, she could call him. But what if his father answered?

"You've changed a lot, too, Alison," Dennis was saying. "You're all grown up."

"Ummph," said Alison. In a minute, she thought, she would just excuse herself and make a break for it. She would say she needed to get a soda.

"In fact," Dennis went on, "unless I'm very much mistaken, you've already got yourself a boyfriend. Am I right? That boy at lunch, huh?"

"He's a friend of mine," Alison said cautiously. She did a quick, frantic scan of the room. Thank God, no parents.

"Uh-huh," said Dennis. His voice was much too loud. "Well, Alison, I've had 'friends' in my time, too." He winked.

"Excuse me," Alison muttered. She fled. She could hear Dennis's laugh, so like her father's, booming behind her. She made it into her bedroom and closed the door.

Was Harry her boyfriend? She didn't know. It wasn't fair. It wasn't fair to have Dennis out there, laughing, probably telling everyone in the family about this before Alison even knew herself. Why couldn't she have any privacy?

It was only five-thirty. People were going to be out there for hours.

She changed into jeans and sneakers and a black T-shirt, carefully hung her dress on a special padded hanger, and covered it with a plastic bag before putting it in the closet. Then she slipped down the hall and out the back door. She grabbed her bike and headed off down the street, standing up as she pedaled to go faster.

"Hey." Along with the whisper, Harry heard the sound of the metal window screen vibrating against its frame under the pressure of something hitting it. "Harry."

Alison. He wheeled over to the window. Beyond the screen, he could just see the top half of her face, and her hand and forearm, upraised to hit the screen. He pushed with his thumbs at the little metal tabs that held the screen in place, released them, forced the screen up, and stuck his head out, looking down to see her standing on the ground under his bedroom window.

"Hey," he said back. He held back a smile. "Um, there is a door." He was amazed at how cool he sounded. Except, like her, he was whispering.

"I didn't want to ring the doorbell," she said. She still had her hair massed on the back of her head in that braid thing.

"Yeah," Harry said. "Well. Do you think you could maybe climb in?"

"Are you nuts?" Even in a whisper, her voice rose on the last word. "Couldn't you just come out?"

"Shhh. It's not that high. You could lean your bike against the wall and stand on it. I'll pull."

After a moment, she shrugged, and went to get the bike. She climbed up on it cautiously, finally managing to balance with one foot on the seat, the other on the handlebars, knees bent, one hand against the wall, the other next to her foot on the handlebars. "Oh, God."

Harry reached out. "Okay. Now walk your hands up the wall. You just need to straighten up enough so you can lean in the window and I can grab you."

"Uh, okay." She didn't move for another minute, and then she did, smoothly, all at once, and Harry grabbed her around the waist, pulling her halfway in. She did the rest herself, landing on the floor where he'd rolled away to make room.

She looked up at him, suddenly shy. "Hi, again."

"Hi." He reached down, and she took his hands. Then he pulled her into his lap again, and looked at her, and kissed her, and it was just like yesterday, only better.

And this time his door was locked.

Long minutes later, Harry pulled a bit away from her. He was panting a little and Alison felt short of breath as well. She put her head down and rested it on his shoulder; she could feel his chest rise and fall with his breathing. He had untucked her T-shirt from her jeans in the back, and his hand was warm there.

"Hey," he said. "Alison?"

"Umm?" She didn't really feel like speaking. It was so nice not to talk. So nice not to think. Just to feel.

"I wanted to ask you..." His voice, low to start, trailed away.

Alison thought, incredulously: is he actually going to ask me to go out with him? She thought of Jason Shepherd and the labyrinthine dating protocol at school and almost giggled. Maybe she'd tell him he'd have to send a message through Felicia Goren. "What?" she prompted.

"I wondered..."

Alison raised her head, looked into Harry's face, tightened her arms around him, and tilted her head inquiringly, waiting for the silly inevitable.

"I just wondered if you knew that I can still have sex," he blurted out. He ducked his head and looked away. "Sort of, that is."

Alison literally felt her jaw drop. She stared at him. Her throat closed up. Her mind went blank.

In the silence, even though she was still on his lap, even though they were still entwined, Alison could feel him separate himself and move apart from her.

"Yes," she said. It came out sort of mangled, and she had to cough a little to clear her throat. She felt her face getting hot. "Yes," she said again, more clearly. "I know."

It took him a moment. "You do," he said, and she could tell by his tone that he wasn't sure whether he should believe her. But at least he was looking at her again, even though she had trouble meeting his gaze.

"I looked it up," Alison said. "At the library." Months before, after the accident, she had chased through a library catalog computer until she found a book whose title and synopsis sounded right. It had had to be special-ordered from a medical library, and, mortified, Alison had buried the title among five additional requests for books from that same library. Spina bifida. Physical therapy for scoliosis. Things like that.

"You looked it up," Harry repeated.

"Yeah." Alison felt a little embarrassed.

He stared at her. She stared right back. And then his mouth twitched at the corner, and so did hers, and they were laughing, choking, pushing their mouths against each other to try to keep the noise down. And when, finally, they stopped, Alison felt Harry's breath against her ear.

"Queen Nerd," he murmured in it. "You are the most incredible Queen Nerd who ever lived."

Alison felt like the Queen of Sheba. She closed her eyes and kissed him again. Then she thought of something, and her eyes opened.

"Harry?" she said. She pulled away a little. "Just because I...I know some kids our age...but I want you to know up front. I'm not ready...I don't plan..." She stumbled into silence, and looked at Harry helplessly. Suddenly she felt nerdy in a way that wasn't good.

But Harry was looking a little surprised. "Well, I'm not ready either," he said. "What did you think?"

Alison blushed. "Well, you did bring it up."

"You looked it up!" he retorted.

Alison turned away. A silence fell. She could feel Harry's palm on the skin of her back, and then, slowly, he slipped it out and reached to make her look at him.

His face was unbelievably serious. And there was an expression on it that she had never seen before.

"Listen, I didn't ask if you knew that I could, uh, make love to you because I wanted us to do it any-time soon...." Now he was a little red, too, avoid-ing her eyes. "I'm only a year older than you are...and it won't...I'm not..."

"Okay," said Alison hurriedly. "I understand."

But Harry hadn't finished. "No," he said. "You don't understand." It took him a moment before he could continue. "There was a reason I asked."

This time, Alison waited.

"I asked because I...I wanted to make sure that you thought of me that way. In a sexual way." And then he looked straight at her, and for the very first time Alison saw that he was a little scared. Of her.

Maybe more than a little.

She looked straight back at him. She thought of the kids at school. They wouldn't think of Harry, of any cripple, as sexual. Probably lots of people wouldn't think of him that way.

"Well," she said, "I do."

HARRY • May

That night, even his father couldn't annoy Harry, though the rabbi was doing his usual routine of shuffling around the kitchen. He kept glancing at Harry when he thought Harry wouldn't notice, and occasionally he lapsed into the distinctive silence that his son knew meant he was conducting a conversation, in his head, with his dead wife. But there were hamburgers for dinner, and Harry had cooked his own so it wasn't overdone, and the Sox would be on TV later. And summer was coming.

If the old man had his own life, in his own universe, well, it didn't matter so much, did it?

Alison was going to improve her basketball game this summer. Or she could pick a sport of her own; Harry didn't want to be dictatorial. Swimming, maybe? They could both do that. And it was a loner's sport, a head sport. Alison might go for it. Truth was, Harry didn't think she'd ever be much of a team player.

You had to face facts, and work with them.

"Harry?"

At first, Harry didn't hear his father. But finally the voice penetrated, and he looked up. "Yeah?" He was a little astonished, and then pleased, that his tone was so relaxed. "What's up?"

"Uh..." The rabbi had not finished his own hamburger. It lay abandoned on his plate. "Adam Shandling did a good job today, don't you think?"

"Yeah," said Harry. "He didn't forget anything. He did okay." Watching his father fidget, he added, deliberately: "Alison thought so, too."

"Oh. Did she?"

"Yeah." Harry waited, but his father let the opening drop. "I'm going to make another hamburger."

"Okay," said the rabbi. Harry could feel his father watching him as he pulled a hamburger patty out of the freezer and wheeled over to the microwave oven to defrost it. At least he wasn't racing around to do things for Harry anymore.

He decided to push his father a little bit. "Yeah, Alison said they were all a little worried he might get distracted or something, but he didn't." He retrieved the patty from the microwave and adjusted his chair to face the stove. "She said her parents were really proud. That's what Alison said." He leaned on the name. He turned on the burner and glanced back at his father.

The rabbi looked very self-conscious. He cleared his throat. "I'm glad to hear that. They said so, of course, earlier today, but—"

"Well, what did you think? That they wouldn't be proud of him?" Harry was swept with a wave of irritation. He was an idiot. He'd actually thought his father was trying to find a way to ask Harry about Alison. But no. His father was still fixated on Adam.

Harry flipped the hamburger over before the first side was done, and had to flip it back.

"You like that girl?" said his father suddenly.

"Who?" said Harry rudely, after a moment. He kept his back to his father. Why should he make it easy for him?

"Alison Shandling." It sounded unexpectedly firm. "Adam's sister. You like her?"

Harry had to fight an unexpected and nearly uncontrollable impulse to snarl, *No!* He almost choked on the word as it struggled to escape from his throat and into the air. He had a sudden memory of a year before, at the synagogue, of his father trying to introduce him to Adam Shandling.

I've met the retard and *his sister*, Harry had said.

He flipped the hamburger again. This time, the first side had burned slightly.

"Yes," he said to the hamburger. "I like her." He squashed the burger flat with the spatula and listened to the sizzling. It would be done in less than a minute. He turned and looked at his father. "I like her a lot."

There was a silence. And then the rabbi said, mildly, "You do realize that she's Jewish?"

There was a stunned moment of absolute silence before Harry burst out laughing. And, incredibly, he heard his father join in.

It was a strange, strained sound, the rabbi's laughter, low and cautious, as if he were afraid someone would hear it and take it away from him.

Harry's hamburger burned beyond repair.

But when the laughter died again into awkwardness, Harry saw that look start to dawn again on his father's face—the Margaret look. The private look.

And Harry felt rage threaten to descend on him again. Before he could think, before he could stop himself, he blurted out, "My mother. Is it true that you met her when you were my age?"

The rabbi's face froze.

"Forget it," Harry said. "Just forget it." He turned off the stove and started to wheel out of the kitchen. "I have some stuff to do—"

"Wait."

Harry paused.

"Yes," said his father. "It's true."

Slowly, Harry wheeled around again.

The rabbi was staring at the table. After a moment, he continued. "I was sixteen."

He stopped, and Harry thought for a moment that that would be all. But then his father went on, speaking slowly.

"My parents picked up your aunt Naomi and me at camp at the end of that summer, and we drove home. I remember my father was wearing a pair of women's white plastic sunglasses that had happened to be in the glove compartment. My mother was in the passenger's seat. She twisted around to ask questions about the summer, the food, the counselors. You know."

Harry didn't—his father had never asked him those questions about camp—but he let it pass.

His father continued. "I was nervous about Naomi. She kept looking at me, and snickering, and I knew it was only a matter of time. And then, when we pulled into a gas station near the state border, she yelled, 'Avi's got a girlfriend!'"

The rabbi shook his head. "I was mortified. I saw my father smile in the rearview mirror. I wanted to disappear."

He stopped for so long that Harry thought he wasn't going to say anything more. Then he went on. "But later, in the driveway at home, when I was helping him wrestle down the trunks, I just told him, out of nowhere, 'She lives in Great Neck. Her name's Margaret.'"

He stopped talking. Harry watched him. The rabbi continued to stare at the table. And then he added, "The other day...when I walked in on you and Alison...I remembered. I remembered talking to my father."

Finally he looked up. "And I wanted you to be able to talk to me."

Harry swallowed. "Well," he said, after a minute, "you need to be able to talk to me, too."

"I know," said the rabbi. He sighed. "It's just that...your mother was the only person it was ever really easy for me to talk to. When she left..."

When she died, Harry thought. But he didn't say it aloud.

"It's hard for me," the rabbi said. He looked at Harry pleadingly. "But I want to try."

You're the only father I have, Harry thought. "We'll try," he said.

ALISON • May

The following Friday evening, Alison didn't get home until after seven. Her parents and Adam had already begun eating without her. Pizza, Alison noticed, from Bertucci's.

"Sorry," she said. She glanced at her parents. Her mother was sitting very straight in her chair, scowling. "We got hung up."

"Diligent of you," said Mrs. Shandling, "on a Friday."

Alison smiled at her uneasily. She slipped into her place at the table. "Oh, yum, eggplant. Adam, can I have that big piece in front of you?"

"I hate eggplant," said Adam.

"Well, the more eggplant I eat, the more cheese there is for you."

"Extra cheese."

"Extra cheese. I stand corrected. No, I *sit* corrected."

"Sit corrected." Adam giggled. "You sit corrected."

Alison watched as Adam carefully loosened a piece from the rest of the pie, using the spatula with one hand while holding his nose with the other. Somehow, he managed to flip the piece onto the plate Alison held out for him.

"It was such a nice day," said Alison chattily. "I love spring."

"I had a nice day too," said Alison's mother. "I had lunch with Rosalie de Silva." She paused meaningfully. "We got caught up."

Alison froze, with her pizza slice midway between the plate and her mouth.

"So, Alison," her mother continued, "why don't you tell us more about this project you've been working on so hard with Paulina? Every afternoon this week, Jake."

"That so?" said the professor. "What's this?"

Alison took a huge bite of her pizza and chewed elaborately. "Ummph," she said.

"I didn't quite catch that," said Mrs. Shandling, distinctly.

Alison looked up then, and met her mother's eyes. She knows about Harry, she thought. A blush slowly rose in her cheeks. She swallowed the food she was chewing and put the slice down on her plate.

"Well?" said her father. "Are you girls getting a start on next fall's science fair?"

Alison's eyes darted to her father. He was clearly sincere. She looked back at her mother and took a deep breath. "This isn't very nice of you," she said.

"I don't think you've behaved very well yourself," her mother snapped back.

"Excuse me?" said Alison's father, looking from one to the other. "What are you talking about?"

"Why don't you tell him?" said Alison quietly to her mother. "Since you know it all."

Mrs. Shandling glared. "Don't you speak to me like that, young lady!"

I can't do this now, Alison thought. She shoved her chair back from the table and jumped up.

"And don't you leave! We're not finished."

Alison paused in the doorway, her back stiff, and then slowly turned around. She crossed her arms in front of her and leaned against the door frame, trembling.

"Please," said the professor, "will both of you calm down and tell me what's going on?"

"Alison won't tell you," said Mrs. Shandling. "But I will." She glared at her daughter. "Alison was not over at Paulina's today, or, in fact, any day this week."

"Oh," said Alison's father blankly.

"That means," Mrs. Shandling went on, "that not only has she been lying to us, but we don't know where she's been or with whom."

The professor turned to Alison. "Well, then, where were you?"

Alison was looking at her mother. You know perfectly well, she thought. She said, "I didn't think I had to account to you for every minute of my life. I thought you trusted me."

"Tell us where you've been," Mrs. Shandling said.

"Is that all you care about?" Alison yelled suddenly. "Where I've been? Don't you care about why? Didn't it ever occur to you to sit me down and ask me how things are going in my life? What I'm thinking about? What's happened lately? That maybe if you asked or showed any interest whatsoever I might tell you?"

"Alison, you're screaming." Mrs. Shandling was on her feet, pointing a finger at Alison, shaking it. "You never scream. It's that boy's influence on you. I know it." Her own voice rose to a shriek.

"Of course we're interested," the professor cut in. He shot his wife a wary glance. "If you and your mother would just calm down—"

"It's all very well for you to be calm," snapped Mrs. Shandling. "I happen to have a very good idea where she's been. She's been with that Harry Roth! I saw how he was looking at her last Saturday at Adam's bar mitzvah. I figured it all out today after Rosalie told me Alison and Paulina had a fight." She turned to Alison. "Over that horrible boy, right?"

There was silence. Adam got up, picked up the box with the extra cheese pizza, and left the kitchen with it. He disappeared into his bedroom down the hall.

"You think you know everything, don't you?" whispered Alison finally. Her face was white.

"Perhaps you'd like to tell me what I've missed?" her mother said.

"What's this about Harry Roth?" asked the professor. He was several minutes behind in comprehension. "Alison, did you have a fight with Paulina?"

"Oh," said Alison, "you have some interest in what I have to say about this?" She was trying not to cry.

"Honey—" Mrs. Shandling started.

"Don't you call me honey!" Alison said. She turned her body away from her mother, toward her father. "Dad. It's nothing to do with Paulina. Paulina's found a friend she likes better than me, but that's not..." She swallowed. "It's Harry Roth. He's my boyfriend. It only just happened. I would have told you"—she shot an angry glance at her mother—"but I wanted to wait awhile. It's a little private."

"Just a minute," said the professor. "You're too young to have a boyfriend!"

"Dad! I'm nearly fifteen!"

"Too young!" Her father was glaring now, too.

Alison clenched her teeth. "I'm going to my room," she said.

"Wait," said her mother. "It's true, then? Harry Roth?" She sounded incredulous.

Alison turned back, slowly, to face her. "Yes," she said distinctly.

"Are you out of your mind?"

Alison suddenly had a blinding headache. "I knew you would never understand," she said.

"You're damned right—"

Alison turned on her heel and ran down the hall to her room.

She could hear them still, though, even from behind a closed door. Not everything, but tones, and the occasional clear word or phrase. She listened hard, still shaking.

Her mother: "Now I've got two kids in the middle of tantrums...." A murmur from her father. Then her mother again, louder, angrier: "You've never been interested...always at the fucking lab..." And her father, equally loud: "You've never goddamned let me—"

Alison stuffed her fingers in her ears. After a few minutes, though, the shouting stopped, and she listened again. There were only undertones now. They'll be here soon, Alison thought. They'll want to talk.

Suddenly, from her mother, she heard distinctly: "She's only just a baby."

Alison froze. No, she thought, with sudden clarity. That's what they don't understand. I've never been a baby. I've never even been a little girl.

After a while, she heard her mother come down the hall. She paused outside Alison's door, but then continued on to Adam's. She went in and began speaking to him.

Alison turned off her light. She slipped under the covers in her clothes. And when her mother finally did knock, she didn't answer.

"I'm sorry," her mother said abruptly to Alison, the next morning. Alison had been standing by the living room window, watching a rabbit hop across the backyard. She swung around. "I'm sorry about yesterday," Mrs. Shandling repeated.

Alison didn't reply. She eyed her mother cautiously, waiting.

"I shouldn't have flown off the handle like that. I guess Harry Roth isn't exactly what I had in mind for your first boyfriend, that's all."

"He's not *your* first boyfriend, he's mine," Alison said. She said it quietly and listened to the sound the words made in the air. Part of her couldn't believe she had said it. "It's not your business," she added.

"I don't agree," said Mrs. Shandling. Her mouth primmed into a tight line. "You're my daughter, and you're only fourteen years old, and I am entitled to an opinion—at the very least—about everything in your life."

Alison tried to recall a subject about which her mother did not have an opinion. "You think you're entitled to an opinion about everything in the world."

"Well, I am," Mrs. Shandling said. "It's the First Amendment."

"Maybe," said Alison. "But does that mean you always have to have a fit about things? Yell and scream at other people? Tell them exactly how right you are and exactly how wrong they are?" Her voice rose. She was making a scene, she thought incredulously. She wasn't being good.

Her mother was breathing hard. "Is that what you think I do?"

"Yes," Alison said defiantly.

"Like when, may I ask?"

"Like yesterday, about Harry."

"I have a goddamned—no, God-given—right to yell and scream about what my daughter is up to. Right now you couldn't possibly understand what I'm talking about, but one day, when you're a mother yourself, you will."

Alison clenched her hands. She fought her impulse to back down. It didn't matter if her mother was right. Alison was right too. "No," she said. "You may have the right to an opinion, but you do not have the right to yell and scream it at me." She felt a surge of power. She was saying what she thought.

She took a deep breath. "And you didn't have the right to scream those things at Rabbi Roth last year. I don't mean the stuff about Adam. I mean the stuff about Harry. And...and the stuff about me. In fact, I shouldn't even have been there. Whether Adam went to Hebrew school had nothing to do with me! It had absolutely nothing to do with me! Why did you make me go? Why did you make me hear those things? Why did you make me see you and Rabbi Roth that way?"

Her mother began, "I thought I apologized—"

Alison cut her off. "It's actually pretty funny, because if I hadn't gone with you that day, I might not be going out with Harry now. But I couldn't believe how you dragged Harry in when you were supposed to be talking about Adam. Just like you dragged me in." She looked up and met her mother's eyes. "Just like you always drag me in with Adam. Just like you always have." She looked down. She discovered she was crying.

"Baby—"

"I'm not a baby! And don't you touch me! Not now. Not until you hear what I have to say." She had a rushing in her ears. She couldn't see very well. She needed a handkerchief.

Somehow there was a box of tissues in front of her. Alison blew her nose. She heard her mother's voice. "I'm listening," it said.

Alison pulled out another tissue and wiped her

eyes. She crumpled the two damp tissues together in her hand. She managed to look up again at her mother. "Please get Daddy," she said. "I want to tell him too, and I don't think I can say this more than once."

Her mother nodded. Alison saw that her eyes were full of worry. I'm sorry, she thought. I never wanted to make trouble, but I have to. She waited.

Quickly, too quickly, her father was there. "Alison, what—" he started, but his wife stopped him with a hand on his arm.

And suddenly they were gone, all the words that not a minute before had been pounding in Alison's head for release. She closed her eyes. She wrapped her arms around herself.

"Is this about Harry Roth again?" said the professor, after a minute or two. "Because I don't care who he is, Alison, you're too young to have a boyfriend. Your mother agrees with me. And that's final."

"Jake—" her mother began.

"No," Alison said. She cleared her throat. "I want to tell you...." She stopped, swallowed. That there's something wrong, she thought. It's about Harry, but it's not. And it's not really about Adam either.

Inevitably, her mother asked, "Is it something about Adam?"

Alison whipped around. "No! It's about me!

It's—it's..." She stopped, stared at her parents.

They stared back. "Honey," her mother said, "we're trying to understand." And when Alison said nothing, she continued, "Sweetheart, look, you're fourteen. It's a difficult time, adolescence. Your emotions just take you over. You're growing up. It's natural you're confused."

"Hormones," said the professor, nodding. "Not your fault. Really nothing you can do."

Alison closed her eyes for a moment. "Just listen to me," she said. "Please just listen."

Her father looked surprised. "Well, we are," he said.

Now or never, Alison thought. Whatever comes out.

She walked to the chair near the sofa, where her parents were sitting, and sat down in it, gingerly, on the edge. She spoke to her hands, twisted together, in her lap. "Well, I am confused, but not the way you think. Not about being fourteen; I know all about that stuff. I know I'm in a stage, but that's not what this is about. And even if it were, you should still listen to me."

"Well, of course," said Alison's mother. "You shouldn't doubt—"

"Shhh," said her father.

Alison flung him a quick, grateful glance before looking down again. "I think," she said, "that I want to talk to you about me. About who I am.

About who I am in this family. About what you expect of me. About what *I* expect of me." She bit her lip. "I guess this part maybe is about Adam, too. There's no way around it; I'm Adam's sister. His twin sister. And...

"And...I've never felt just like me, just like Alison. I can't be myself in this family because it's more important that I be...this person who's not Adam. Who's normal. Smart. Good. Who's not..." She paused, swallowed. "Who's not autistic."

"Honey, that's absolutely—"

"I'm telling you how I feel!" Alison shouted, at one of them, at both of them, she wasn't sure; she didn't know who'd spoken, and she didn't care. "Don't you see when it comes to this, it doesn't matter how you feel? What I think is what matters right now! Can't you see that?"

There was silence. Alison got up abruptly and reached for the tissue box. She busied herself blowing her nose again. After a while, she heard her mother's voice.

"Alison? Are you saying...do you really mean that you think we love you only because you're not autistic like Adam?"

"Alison?" said her father.

"I'm not saying you realize it," said Alison quietly. She was suddenly filled with despair. They would deny it. Of course they would.

"Oh, God," said Alison's mother.

Even if He's there, thought Alison, He's not going to help. She poked with one finger at a small hole in the knee of her jeans. We're on our own. There was silence. And, then, in it, she heard a peculiar, snorting, wrenching noise, and looked up.

Her father was crying. Her mother had her arms around him, her body against his, her cheek on his head. But her face was toward Alison, and it was frightened and wrinkled and old.

I am a horrible human being, thought Alison. She tightened up, became as small as possible in the chair. "I'm sorry," she mumbled to her knees. She thought her parents could not hear her, but her voice would not get louder. "I'm so sorry." She wished she could be somewhere else. She wished she had not started. Why had she thought it was so important? There were children starving in India. In Boston. There were kids whose parents beat them. Or worse.

Did it matter why you were loved? So long as you were? She listened to her father sob. Why didn't he stop?

Then he did. "Alison," he said. And again, "Alison." It wasn't his voice at all. And then, when she dared look again, she watched him disentangle himself from his wife and get up and leave the room.

Alison's mother got up too. She stood uneasily by the sofa for a second and then advanced and put her hand on Alison's shoulder. "We'll talk more about this," she said. "Honey?" Awkwardly, she knelt next to the chair and put her arms around Alison. "We love you, honey. We do." Her arms tightened. "We just have to find some way to explain... love isn't simple."

Alison thought of Harry. "I know that," she said. Her voice croaked.

"Oh, honey," said Alison's mother. Alison could hear that she, too, was near tears. "You only think you do. Love gets worse when you get older. It gets even more complicated." And then she was gone.

Alison stayed, alone, in the chair. She wondered how she would feel if Harry cried.

Dinner that night was brief. Alison almost didn't join the rest of them. She had a headache. She wasn't hungry. But Adam came to her door and stood there and looked at her. "There are french fries," he said, and waited, and finally Alison went with him to the table.

Her mother was there, but not her father. She went out of her way to give Alison another hug, and Alison felt a little better, but not much. "Your father is in the den," Alison's mother said. "He's trying to write you a letter."

"Oh," said Alison. She took a small bite from her casserole. "He doesn't need to write a letter." The pounding in her head increased. She watched Adam make a house, stacking the fries as if they were Lincoln Logs. "It's okay. Can we just forget it?"

Her mother shook her head. "Alison? Do you...do you feel like you're"—she glanced at Adam—"just Alison, just yourself, when you're with other people? Like Paulina? I know you're not such good friends nowadays. But before? Didn't you feel Paulina liked you for yourself?"

Alison closed her eyes, and then opened them. "Maybe," she said slowly. "I'm not sure." She paused. Slowly, she added, "But I don't think I felt...entirely like myself when I was with her. She was always someone who didn't mind about Adam. That was always more important."

"Oh," said her mother.

There was silence. And into it, desperately, Alison found herself saying, "But with Harry, I'm just me. I don't know why. But I am."

"Oh," said her mother again.

Alison stood up. "I'm not very hungry," she said. "I think I'll go back to my room."

Alison went to bed early, but not to sleep. She lay stiff in bed, holding her stuffed crab, Josephine, replaying everything she had said, everything they had said. She could see the hall light; it was a bar of white under her door. They were still up; occasionally she heard a murmur. Finally, hours later, she heard them outside her door. There was a whisper of paper. And a minute later, the hall light went off and she heard their bedroom door close.

She sat up in bed and turned on her bedside lamp. There was an envelope on the floor near the door. After a moment, she went and got it, and climbed back into bed with it. She held it between her hands for a moment, and then reached into her night table drawer for the flashlight. She turned off the lamp and got way under the covers with the letter, the circle of light from the flashlight, and Josephine.

She opened the envelope and took out the pages. They were written out in longhand. She recognized her father's writing on the first sheet.

Dear Alison,

We do love you. I love you. Your mother has told me that you understand that love is complex. But it's simple, too, and what I feel for you began before you were born and long before you were who you are today. Maybe it's just biology, but fathers love their daughters, and it doesn't much matter who they are. Your mother doesn't want me to say this, but I love you because you're my daughter and that's all there is to it. That's rule number one. And Adam is my son, and I love him, and that's all there is to that, too.

But I also understand that, at least in our family, it isn't really that simple. You said you felt that you were just the one who wasn't autistic. Well, I am very, very, very glad you're not. I can't apologize for that. I can't tell you how surprised I was to hear you say that you felt we didn't love you for you. That was always so easy. The hardest thing for me has been learning to love your brother for who he is. But you—Alison, for me the whole world always lit up every time you smiled at me and called me Daddy. Maybe it was sweeter because your brother didn't. In fact, I know it was. But I don't know what to do about that. I've been staring at this paper trying to think of what else to say, and coming up empty. I'm afraid I can't help you. I don't know how.

I love you enough, and I respect you enough, to be honest with you, Alison. I don't know what else to do, at least not right now. Maybe later.

Love,
Daddy

The handwriting became her mother's.

Darling Alison,
I'm not like your father. We'd do better to talk, face-to-face, and I hope we can do that soon. But I wanted to have part of this letter, too. To say what I could to help you now. I wish I could help more.

You know that we were very shocked at what you said this afternoon. I have thought since that maybe I shouldn't have been.

You're right, in a way. You and Adam are twins, and from the time that we first noticed Adam was different, we've measured his progress against yours. You were cuddly; he wasn't. You talked; he didn't. It was so clear that he needed us more than you did. I look back, and I see that we've spent far, far less time with you than with your brother. So maybe it was inevitable that you'd come to believe we love you only because you're normal. It's the thing you've seen us focus on.

But, honey, it's not true. I just don't know how to convince you. I've thought and thought. I hope I'll find the right words later, when we talk. I don't have them now. I'm sorry.

Something else. You mentioned that you don't like it when I yell and scream about my opinions. I'm sorry that it upsets you. But what I think I would like is if you would yell and scream back. Like today. I'm proud of you, honey. I'm proud that you stood up and told us what you were feeling. I think it's one of the most important things that happened today. That was you being you, wasn't it? I don't remember you ever letting go like that before. You've been hiding how you felt from us, but not anymore. So I think you can be you—just you—in our family. It's already beginning.

About Harry. I do feel uncomfortable about him. It's hard for me to forget the past. And you're very young. I'd like us to talk about boys sometime. You probably don't want to, but I insist. I suppose if Harry helps you feel good about being yourself, then I will try to get used to him. I can't promise more than that.

Let me know when you're ready to talk. It doesn't have to be right away. Whenever you're ready.

What your father said about love and children. That goes for me too, honey. So much.

Love,

Mom

P.S. I hope this helps.

It did help, Alison thought. It did help some, even though she knew that they still didn't understand, not fully. And maybe never would.

They had their own worlds, separate from hers, and they understood things differently. But they did love her, their way. It was something. Maybe it was enough.

It would have to be.

And, anyway, tomorrow she would see Harry.